In the heat of battle.

We had been overrun. In the distance, in the direction of the bunkered hill, fierce fighting continued; battles that I could not see were being fought. More Russians were passing by every minute. I heard them; I saw them scrambling through the trench.

I was trapped behind enemy lines.

If discovered, I would be killed. Even playing dead would not save me; even dead, once found, I would be skewered on the end of a bayonet.

I had only one chance, I knew, to save myself.

The dead eyes of the blond Russian boy seemed to be watching me. With my fingers, I closed the lids. Strange though it may seem, I did not want him looking at me and at what I was about to do.

◆ ◆ ◆

"X's first-person narrative screams the horrors of war: the gruesome carnage and the confusion and terror. This fierce yell for peace is based on the histories of two survivors and of many more survivors, now forgotten."   —*Booklist*

"Survival stories set in war-torn Europe are not uncommon; what makes this one noteworthy is its unusual perspective."
                                                           —*The Horn Book*

DISCARDED FROM
GARFIELD COUNTY PUBLIC
LIBRARY SYSTEM

WINNER OF THE CHRISTOPHER AWARD

A BCCB BLUE R

AN ALA

GA
Par
244
Para
(97(
www
D0401471

OTHER SPEAK BOOKS

SOLDIER X

DON WULFFSON

speak

An Imprint of Penguin Group (USA) Inc.

*For their guidance, support, and invaluable insight,
the author wishes to thank Tom Tarter, Christian Goodell,
Bob Kagan, John Vasile, and (most especially)
his editor, Jill Davis.*

SPEAK
Published by Penguin Group
Penguin Group (USA) Inc.,
345 Hudson Street, New York, New York 10014, U.S.A.
Penguin Books Ltd, 80 Strand, London WC2R ORL, England
Penguin Books Australia Ltd, 250 Camberwell Road, Camberwell, Victoria 3124, Australia
Penguin Books Canada Ltd, 10 Alcorn Avenue, Toronto, Ontario, Canada M4V 3B2
Penguin Books (N.Z.) Ltd, 182-190 Wairau Road, Auckland 10, New Zealand

First published in the United States of America by Viking,
a division of Penguin Putnam Books for Young Readers, 2001
Published by Speak, an imprint of Penguin Group (USA) Inc., 2003

1 3 5 7 9 10 8 6 4 2

Copyright © Don L. Wulffson, 2001
All rights reserved

THE LIBRARY OF CONGRESS HAS CATALOGED THE VIKING EDITION AS FOLLOWS:
Soldier X / Don L. Wulffson.
p. cm.
"Based on a true story."
Summary: In 1943 sixteen-year-old Erik experiences the horrors of war when
he's drafted into the German army and sent to fight on the Russian front.
ISBN: 0-670-88863-X
I. World War, 1939–1945—Campaigns—Soviet Union—Fiction.
[1. World War, 1939–1945—Campaigns—Soviet Union.] I. Title.
PZ7.W96373 So 2001 [Fic]—dc21 99-04918

Printed in the United States of America
Set in Times New Roman

Speak ISBN 0-14-250073-9

Except in the United States of America, this book is sold subject to the condition that
it shall not, by way of trade or otherwise, be lent, re-sold, hired out, or otherwise
circulated without the publisher's prior consent in any form of binding or cover
other than that in which it is published and without a similar condition
including this condition being imposed on the subsequent purchaser.

For Pamela
My Wife, My Love, My Best Friend

Prologue

My name is Erik Brandt. I live near Seattle, Washington, in a small house in a wooded area overlooking a lake. I like the woods; they are quiet and make for a pleasant place to write. I also hate them. They bring back dark memories of battles fought long ago.

Most of my friends and acquaintances in the area call me Erik, or Professor, or Dr. Brandt. Though none of them know it, I prefer a different name. I prefer to be called X. It is simply a letter, but it has far more meaning to me than my real name.

I am no longer a young man. My once sharp blue eyes are now faded, and I need to wear reading glasses. My hair, once blond, is now steel gray, and I wear it long. My once boyish, peach-fuzz face is now bearded. The beard covers the scars on my face, put there when a machine-gun bullet went into my open mouth and out my left cheek. I walk with a bit of a limp, the result of being hit in the knee by a large piece of shrapnel when I was sixteen. I wear a prosthesis—an artificial arm and hand. I lost my left arm above the elbow—and received my other wounds and injuries—during the Second World War.

After the War, I became a history teacher. As a teacher, one of the first things my students always noticed was my prosthesis. I'd see fear and revulsion in their eyes, but also a great deal of curiosity. In answer to their unspoken question, and to put the matter to rest, I simply told my students that I lost my arm during the Second World War. "During the fighting in Germany I was hit by a machine-gun bullet just above the elbow," I would tell them. But though they clearly wanted me to, I would never tell them more.

"It must have been terrifying fighting the Nazis," I remember one of my students saying to me after class one day. "But the Nazis—the Germans—were out to conquer the world. Somebody had to stop them!"

The boy seemed to look up to me as some sort of hero. And like all of my students, he made an incorrect assumption about my role in the war. He assumed I had been an American GI fighting the Germans.

I never told him—or any of my students—that it was the other way around. During World War II, I was a German soldier.

Part One

In Dead Men's Clothes

March 21, 1944

I can still smell the stench of the troop train. I can still feel myself sway with the motion of it as it pounded eastward from Germany toward the battlefields of Russia.

The train was old, a relic that had been pressed into service because of the war. Once elegant, and used perhaps for wealthy people going on vacation, time had rendered it into something ornately decrepit. Filthy gold tassels hung from faded green velvet curtains; the windows were oval in shape, the glass yellowed by age; stuffing sprouted from seats upholstered in cracking, scaly-looking leather; and at the back of the car, behind a curtained-off alcove, was a toilet that emptied directly onto the tracks.

Like myself, most of those on the train were young boys—teenagers. Other than being soldiers in the German army, we had little in common. Fear, uncertainty, and homesickness—these were the only real bonds that united

3

us. We were also alike in that we wore dead men's clothes. By truck and rail, the boots and gray-green uniforms of those killed in battle had been returned to Germany for washing and mending. The sleeves of my jacket had jagged little rips that had been painstakingly sewn, and my shirt collar had dark bloodstains all the way around. I found myself wondering about the soldier who had died in the uniform. I wondered who he had been and how he had been killed. Would I, too, die in the uniform? Would it then be passed along to another boy, someone who would then wonder about me, about who I had been?

The train carrying us toward the front lines departed early that morning from Nuremberg, Germany. It was March 21, 1944, my sixteenth birthday. I told no one. The fact that it was my birthday was of no importance, except to me.

"You are nothing—your Volk *are everything."*

That was a motto of the Hitler *Jugend,* or HJ, the Hitler Youth. For five years the words had been drilled into my head; but not until sitting there on the troop train, amidst all the others, had I felt them so keenly: I was nothing; I did not matter. According to Adolf Hitler, only my country mattered.

"You were born to die for Germany."

In 1939, Hitler declared membership in the *Jugend* mandatory. Parents who objected were imprisoned; some were hanged. I had no choice. I volunteered for service. Only my father—who had died when I was a baby—was

German. My mother and grandparents were Russian; with forged papers, they had emigrated illegally to Germany in the late 1920s. They had learned to speak German fluently and without accent; they had renovated an old house, turning the downstairs into a restaurant, the upstairs into our living quarters; they paid taxes. In every way that really mattered, they had become good German citizens. Nevertheless, should the SS, the *Schutzstaffel,* discover their background, they would have been deported, perhaps killed.

When I joined the Hitler Youth, Austria and Czechoslovakia had already been annexed by Germany—to create what Hitler called *Lebensraum,* living space for the German people. On September 1, 1939, World War II began in earnest; on that day, we invaded Poland. It fell to us in sixteen short days. Denmark, Norway, Belgium, Luxembourg, and France—by 1940, all had fallen. Clearly, no longer was it *Lebensraum* that Hitler desired—it was all of Europe, and then the world.

Early in the war, one of our allies had been Russia— known then as the Soviet Union. The alliance had been an uneasy one: Russia, under the leadership of Stalin, was a Communist country; Hitler was anti-Communist, and it was well known that he did not trust Stalin any more than Stalin trusted him. On June 22, 1941, we attacked Russia as well.

A cloud of confusion settled over our home. My mother and grandparents now lived in terror of being found out. And I felt greatly torn. By birth, I was half

Russian. Yet Germany was my country, and I wore the uniform of the Hitler Youth—the black pants, brown shirt, and red armband.

Before the invasion of Russia, all had seemed so simple. I had enjoyed most of the activities of the *Jugend*—the sports, the camp-outs, the physical fitness programs, even the military training, which consisted mostly of target practice. Best of all were the dances and other get-togethers with the girls' branch of the *Jugend,* the *Bund Deutscher Mädchen* (League of German Girls).

Upon entering the Hitler Youth, we were given a choice of entering different groups within the organization. Those interested in flying, for example, would apply for the *Flieger-HJ* (the flying youth). My choice was *Die Sprache-HJ,* in which we studied language; essentially, we were being prepared to become interrogators or spies. My French and English were passable; however, having been raised in a household where Russian was spoken with as much ease and facility as German, it was in Russian that I excelled. Our teacher, Herr Kraus, was quite good. Still, he sometimes made errors in his pronunciation, inflection, and use of idiomatic expression. I held my tongue. Correcting one's teacher was simply not done.

And one kept quiet about the torture and murder of Jews, foreigners, Communists—and everyone else the Nazis considered "undesirables." The inevitable consequence of criticizing the government was simply to become just one more undesirable. In my hometown of

Vilsburg, a man named Zoll spoke out against the invasion of Russia. His tongue was cut out; then he and three suspected communists were hanged. And then there was "the death bus." Painted a ghastly green—including its windows—it was in the woods, some twenty kilometers or so from Vilsburg. Cripples and mental defectives were taken to the thing and put to death, gassed. And thrown in with them was a Lutheran minister—who'd publicly protested the hideous practice.

To the horror of all Germans, in 1940 the bombing of our country began. Each year it got worse. By 1943 some of our cities lay in ruins. Food, gasoline, and numerous other goods were in short supply and strictly rationed. Our days of easy conquests were long since over; the British, Americans, and Russians held firm against our forces, then began to attack. Suddenly we were on the defensive, and very afraid.

From the battlefields, especially those of Russia, maimed and crippled German soldiers returned with blank, dead stares. Though the newspapers told only of "minor setbacks," the tales told by soldiers were very different. They spoke of horror, slaughter, and retreat on the Eastern Front. Minsk, Kiev, Kharkov, Donetz, Belgorod— in these places and others, tens of thousands of our men were killed. Whole companies of the *Wehrmacht,* our army, literally ceased to exist.

I was eleven when the war had started. With my friends, enthralled, the hair on the back of my neck standing up, I had watched parades as rank after rank of soldiers of the *Wehrmacht* passed in review, the cheers of the onlookers drowned out by the thundering footfalls of their hob-nailed jackboots. How powerful they had looked! How fearsome! How invincible!

At the time, I had felt cheated. I dreamed of being one of them. A hero. In my mind, I saw myself leading an attack on an enemy position. Single-handedly, I would destroy it. But then I would be wounded—most likely in the shoulder. Beautiful nurses would take care of me. Officers would pin medals on me, praise my courage, and thank me for what I had done for my country.

In April of 1944, males sixteen years of age were declared eligible to fight. I was sick with terror. That I was only fifteen did not matter. "By the date of your birth, I see," said a very fat little *Feldwebel*—sergeant—at the induction center, "you will be sixteen by the time you reach wherever it is you are to go." He studied my records. "And undoubtedly your command of the Russian language will land you a spot as an interrogator, or cause you to be used in some similar capacity." He banged the word ELIGIBLE on my papers with a rubber stamp, dismissed me, then gestured for the next boy in line to step forward.

Thus it was that I found myself on a troop train headed to war. As it screamed across the landscape, I kept thinking there must be some mistake, that this could not really be happening. I wanted to get off. I wanted to go home.

The train thundered onward.

Guided Tour

Sitting next to me was a freckle-faced boy named Jakob. He jabbered a lot, at first about his family and their business. His father, he told me, was an apple dealer and was often traveling. He would buy up orchards in the spring when the flowers were on the trees; then as the apples ripened, Jakob and his sisters would pick and pack them. "Our apples are shipped all over Germany," he told me proudly.

"My father died of influenza when I was a baby," I told Jakob. "I'm an only child, and I live with my mother and her parents—my grandparents—in an apartment above our restaurant in Vilsburg."

Jakob looked at me expectantly, as though I had more to tell. But there was really nothing of interest to say, and talking about my family only made me more homesick, especially for my mother. When she had seen me off at the train station in Nuremberg that morning, she had looked shrunken and shriveled, and wore dark clothes, like a mourner at a funeral—mine.

Jakob plucked an undersized booklet from the breast pocket of his jacket. In its pages, filled with maps and tourist information, he seemed to find a refuge from reality. Shortly, he began reading aloud from it as we traveled eastward, across Germany and into Czechoslovakia. The train slowed as it passed through Prague.

"Prague is the capital of Czechoslovakia," he told me. "We have now traveled 120 kilometers east from Nuremberg."

As he rattled on about the history and wonders of Prague, I looked out and saw a dreary city that had become a supply depot and garrison for our troops. I wished my self-appointed tour guide would be quiet.

I didn't feel very well. The train had become increasingly hot and stuffy; my face was wet with perspiration and my uniform clung damply to my body. My head ached, and the stench coming from the open toilet, only a few steps behind where I sat, was making me nauseous. At the moment, the history of Prague held very little interest for me.

Perhaps an hour and a half later, the train again slowed as it clacked through Kraków, Poland. Our bombing raids had gutted whole sections of the city. We passed one long street on which a blackened body hung from almost every streetlight.

"Partisans," I heard someone say.

Jakob—the "tour guide"—was too immersed in his booklet to see the horrid sight. "At the center of Kraków is what is known as the Old City," he droned on, "a fortress, which, during the thirteenth century, was moated and walled." He glanced out the window for a moment, then returned his attention to his book. "Next, we should be passing Tarnów, Poland." He shrugged rounded shoulders. "But after that, well, it is anyone's guess."

Not even my travel guide knew exactly where we were headed. Our commanders kept us in the dark about our destination, so we simply sat—bored and scared—as the train raced across Poland toward the war.

As I have said, most of the forty or so soldiers in the car, like me, were new conscripts. We did not know each other, nor had we even trained together. Other than target practice in the *Jugend*, there had only been three short weeks of actual military training. During this time I learned how to march, salute, how to say "yes, sir" and "no, sir," and how not to question orders. Because ammunition was in short supply, I was taught how to assemble, load, and clean a Mauser rifle, but only rarely was I allowed to fire one. I tossed practice grenades at wooden cutouts of soldiers. That, then, was the extent of my preparation for war, as it was for the other boys on the train.

There was also a handful of veterans on the train, many of whom had been wounded, treated, and now were being sent back to battle. Most just sat quietly, grim expressions on their faces. But one, a man of about thirty or so, kept wandering around the car. When Jakob got up and made his way to the curtained-off alcove, the toilet, the veteran decided to take his seat. He picked up the boy's pack and began going through it. When Jakob returned, it was to find the veteran enjoying a sandwich he had found in the pack.

"This is quite good," said the veteran. "Did your mamma make it for you?"

Stunned, my freckle-faced tour guide didn't know what to do or say.

Across the aisle I saw other boys looking on, their expressions both curious and apprehensive.

The veteran eating the sandwich was not an especially big man, but there was something terribly frightening about him, something murderous, and there was no question that he would have his way. He tossed Jakob his pack and rifle. Red-faced, humiliated, Jakob made his way down the aisle, in search of a place to sit.

Pickles and Knackwurst. That is what was in the sandwich the man was eating. He kept his eyes on me as he ate, sending chills down my spine. When he was done, he wiped his hands on my shirt, as though it was quite a natural thing to do. "I lost these at Stalingrad." He held up his left hand. The last three fingers were missing. "Now they are sending me back to Russia. I don't think that's fair, do you?"

"No," I replied, keeping my voice as steady as I could.

"It is not just because of my fingers that I should not be sent back. It is because a man can endure only so much! The bombing, the artillery—especially the artillery!" For a long moment he lapsed into silence. "Perhaps they are sending me back because they know that I will not die—because I have the power, the strength. I can take care of myself." He looked me squarely in the eye. "Do you sense my power, boy?"

"Yes."

He nodded, grinning with self-satisfaction. "You are going to love Russia!" He launched into a litany of horror stories. The worst was about partisans—men, women, and children who fought us in small, roving bands and who had sabotaged a troop train like ours on the way to the front. "There were bodies and parts of bodies everywhere," he told me with seeming glee. "Mostly they were just *kinder*—stupid children—like you. Never even got a chance to fire their rifles!"

With that, he got up, belched, and wandered off, probably in search of others to torment—leaving me scared to death and sure our train would blow up at any moment.

A while later, Jakob returned to his seat beside me. His booklet was in his pocket; he sat rigidly, in silence, staring out the window as foreign landscape flashed by. Much of it was serene, pretty. But then Jakob pointed, horror in his eyes. I turned in time to see a church that had been set up as a temporary hospital. A wooden cart was headed away from the place, in the direction of a deep trench. It was being pulled by men, not horses, and it was filled to overflowing with corpses.

Criminals?

The next afternoon we reached the town of Gryuskow, Poland, about thirty kilometers from the Russian border. Though seemingly undamaged, the town was strangely deserted.

Lugging our packs and rifles, we debarked the train. *Feldwebels*—sergeants—formed us into ranks and marched us—more than three hundred of us—across open fields. Thistle burrs caught in our pants; underbrush scraped our legs.

The sky was turning dark and a wind gusted as we approached a huge, defunct factory of some sort. It was out in the middle of nowhere, and I could only guess what had had once been made there. Perhaps lumber had been processed; the first shed we passed, a large, open-air affair of corrugated tin and wood supports, housed a large band saw. Farther on were several other sheds. In all of them were piles of warped boards, except for one in which there was a kind of dredging machine with a string of rusty scoops.

Criminals?

"Achtung! Stillgestanden!"

At the command of our *Feldwebels,* we stopped, then quickly snapped to attention in front of the enormous building. Seeming on the verge of collapse, it sagged in the middle and was tilted to one side; its tin roof was half eaten away by rust.

After a long wait, we were ordered forward into the building. Inside, the place was shadowy, freakish. Dead, monstrous machinery towered. Outside, the wind picked up. The roof rattled and banged. An electric generator whirred. Bare bulbs draped overhead gave everything a spooky quality, like some kind of badly lit nightmare. And there were nightmare people in there with us. Not far from where I put down my pack and bedroll was a crew of skeletons. Emaciated, heads shaven, wearing striped, pajamalike garments, they waited to serve us, standing behind steaming kettles set out on large wooden crates. Most had yellow Stars of David sewn onto their ragged, dirty clothes, marking them as Jews.

"Achtung!" The master sergeant called for attention. "With your mess kits, lineup! Quickly! *Schnell!*"

My God, this is what we are doing to our own countrymen? Is this the Germany we are fighting for?

I waited my turn in line, each step taking me closer to the people. Never before had I seen human beings in such condition.

Eyes downcast, an old man handed me a quarter loaf of black bread. A girl who could not have been more than nine or ten ladled soup into my outstretched mess tin. I thanked her.

"Danke," I said.

Her response was an attempted grin so rigid it seemed it would crack her face open.

I returned to my place and ate without appetite. Jakob spotted me and asked if he could join me.

"Yes, of course," I said, glad for the company.

A moment later, a tall, gangly boy, who I would later learn was named Oskar, joined Jakob and me. The three of us ate in silence, as did most in that strange, cavernous building. Still there was an undertone of voices. Behind us was another group of boys. In a nasal voice, one was declaring that the Jews across the way were an "exception," that most Jews, as we had been told by the government, had simply been "relocated" to work camps and were well treated.

I wanted to believe this—perhaps we all did. But deep down I knew that those people were no exception.

"This bunch must be criminals," the nasal voice continued.

"Do you think that's true, that they're criminals?" Jakob asked.

"I don't know," I replied. "I don't think I know much of anything anymore."

"I hope they *are* criminals," said Oskar. Large eyes in a narrow face blinked. "Because if they are not, then we are."

Baptism of Fire

At dawn, after a meal of weak tea and hard rolls, we were issued additional ammunition and ordered outside. *Feld-webels* organized us into squads. Jakob, Oskar, and I were assigned to the 7th Platoon of the 14th Squad of the Fourth *Landser* (Infantry) Division. There were nineteen of us in the platoon: one medic, fifteen recruits, and three veterans. A man named Dobelmann, a *Feldwebel,* was our platoon leader. He sickened and terrified me.

War had turned his face into something grotesque, hideous. He looked as though he were wearing a fright mask. He was missing one ear, and only a small flap of the other remained. His entire face was an impossible jigsaw puzzle of scars.

As did most *Feldwebels,* he wore a whistle around his neck. He blew it. He ordered us into line and to attention, then commanded us to stand at "parade rest." We slammed our rifle butts to the ground; then, with a straight, rigid arm, each soldier held his rifle by the barrel at an angle to his right leg. Dobelmann strode down our ranks, talking to us in turn.

"Do I frighten you, son?" he demanded of one recruit.

"No, sir!" came the shouted response.

"He's a liar, isn't he?" he yelled at the next boy.

"Yes, sir. I mean, no, sir! I mean, I don't know, sir!"

"Yes, you don't know what you mean," said Dobelmann evenly.

He strode past several more recruits, staring each in the eye. He stopped next to me, in front of Oskar. Oskar was so tall and skinny that Dobelmann had to look up at him; still, it was to him that he spoke directly, at the same time delivering a speech to the whole platoon. "I am not here to frighten you." His voice softened. "I am here to save your lives—and even your pretty faces." He attempted a smile. It came out crooked. "Do exactly as I tell you at all times. I cannot guarantee anything—except that I will increase your chances of surviving this war. You are going to be facing men who are going to try to kill you. You must kill them first—to save yourself and the men beside you." He stepped back a pace. He raised his voice. "And you are here to defend your country—for it is now *we* who are on the defensive. You are here to protect your parents, your brothers and sisters, your grandparents— your people, your *Volk*. They are depending on you. If the Bolsheviks—the Russian Communist pigs—break through, then they will win the war, and horror beyond imagining will befall Germany, your homeland." He nodded. "That is all," he said. "Fall out."

More trucks and other vehicles arrived. We prepared to board, awaiting the order. Another whistle squealed; then the voice of an *Obergefreiter,* a lance corporal, bellowed.

"Achtung!"

Three hundred pairs of heels clicked together. Rifles clattered in unison as the entire company snapped to attention, ramrod straight.

In the black uniform of the SS, an overweight, bespectacled officer made his way to the forefront and addressed us, his voice loud and high-pitched: "You will be reinforcing and resupplying the 15th Rifle Corps of the Fourth Division at Tarnapol, in the Soviet Union. The Fourth Division has suffered heavy casualties, and battalion headquarters there remains under siege. For almost three months we have held firm and repelled the Russian assaults. But our men are malnourished and running low on munitions. It is your job to help reinforce our troops there and to bring in badly needed supplies. Be alert at all times. Contingents of the Russian army and partisans will undoubtedly be encountered on the road ahead. *Heil* Hitler!" He saluted rather indifferently, then, hands behind his back, ambled off as if he were suddenly going for a walk, deep in thought. He stopped, turned, and looked at all of us. Then he spoke loudly: "And may God be with you!"

Our platoon climbed aboard the trucks. The canvas sidings were rolled up and tied, and benches were secured to the bed of the vehicle with steel support rods. Wooden crates of supplies went under the seats and in a line down the aisle between the seats. Dobelmann and two other veterans climbed aboard, the three of them hefting a heavy-caliber machine gun and long belts of ammunition. Behind the cab of the truck, the two set the weapon onto a rotating mount. The other trucks in the column were being similarly equipped.

As they worked, arming and locking down the machine gun, I stared at the back of Dobelmann's head. On the back of his scalp was a saucer-size area where little hair grew. The skin was bright pink and wrinkled, and from the folds of the wrinkles sprouted a few black hairs and round, spongy-looking lumps of flesh.

Looking at the man made me ill. I sat down on one of the hard wooden benches, averting my gaze from him. Jakob and I and some of the other boys exchanged glances, silently communicating our revulsion. I did not know it, of course, nor did any of us, that we would soon be seeing things a thousand times worse.

The convoy snaked across the landscape on rutted dirt roads. In the truck, we sat stiffly. All of us were about the same age, except for Dobelmann, who was manning the machine gun behind the cab, and the other two veterans.

Sick with fear, we just sat there, rifles clamped between our knees, rocking with the motion of the truck. Rather than soldiers, we looked like prisoners condemned to death.

The only one of our platoon who seemed unafraid was an athletic-looking boy named Meyer Fassnacht. I heard him say repeatedly that he looked forward to battle. To him, it was all just a grand adventure. He seemed genuinely unafraid.

Our truck carried crated supplies, as did many others. Some trucks carried no passengers, only munitions, piled high under heavy tarpaulins. At the front, rear, and middle of the convoy were armored vehicles, all equipped with fifty-millimeter cannon. Our highest ranking officers rode in Steiners, Jeeplike vehicles. Traveling alongside the trucks and armored cars were two motorcycles, both of which had a sidecar for a passenger, usually a veteran soldier with a sub-machine gun.

Though we saw no sign of the enemy, we did begin to see evidence of war—of battles and bombings. We passed through several small towns, most of them in ruins. Wrecked vehicles, both civilian and military, lay alongside the road. The oddest of these was a Mercedes-Benz convertible. It lay sort of sideways in a pool created by a bomb crater, its back seat filled with brown water in which a quacking duck paddled around.

The few road signs changed from Polish to Cyrillic; we had entered Russia. Off to our right were low, humpbacked mountains; all else was unbroken flatland, much of it charred black. The air smelled of burned wheat—almost like overdone toast.

A platter-faced young soldier sitting near the front of the truck got up the nerve to ask Dobelmann about what we were seeing—and smelling. He turned his jigsaw puzzle of a face in our direction.

"Before they retreat, the Ivans burn their fields, all their farms and crops, and butcher whatever livestock they cannot take with them. They leave nothing."

"What's an Ivan?" a boy with rosy cheeks next to me asked.

"A Russian," I told him.

"But why do they call them Ivans?"

I explained that Ivan was a common first name in Russia. But by the perplexed expression on the boy's face I could see he was struggling with the concept. I tried again to explain. Again, he did not get it. His thick-wittedness annoyed me, and I did not explain further. But Rosy Cheeks was not done with me yet. "They also call them Soviets. How come?" he asked.

I explained that Russia was part of the Soviet Union. "The Soviet Union is a Communist country. Russia is one of the so-called republics."

"I don't understand," said Rosy Cheeks.

"Yes, I can see that," I said sarcastically, and leaned back and closed my eyes.

A moment later Rosy Cheeks asked another question.

I did not answer. My face uplifted to the sun, I feigned sleep. The annoying questions finally stopped. I was dozing, thinking about home, when I became aware of a strange droning noise. It sounded like it was overhead, and seemed to be getting closer. At the sudden eruption of yelling and the chatter of machine-gun fire my eyes flipped open.

"Polikarpovs!" someone yelled.

Small Russian fighter planes were plummeting toward us. I could see the pilots in the open-cockpit planes and the red-orange blasts of gunfire as they strafed our convoy. With resounding *bangs,* holes were punched in the metal of the trucks; powder-puffs of dust popped up from the road; the rosy-cheeked boy screamed and grabbed his face as hot liquid exploded from the back of his head, drenching me.

"What do I do?"

It was me that screamed this, as I frantically wiped at the gore on me.

A munitions truck ahead of us ruptured and disintegrated in flames.

Our truck veered wildly to the right. A tire blew.

"Out!" screamed jigsaw-puzzle face. Gripping the machine gun mounted behind the cab, Dobelmann's entire body was vibrating as he fired at the planes. "Get out of the truck, boys!" he yelled again as the heavy vehicle cracked through saplings and slammed to an abrupt stop in a culvert.

It seemed to take a century to get out of that truck.

A few soldiers scrambled over the sides. I tried to go

with them, but Jakob was pushing me from behind. I stumbled over the crates between the seats, then found myself in a logjam of bodies, a tangled crush of scared kids all trying to get out the back of the truck at the same time.

"Move!"

I screamed the word in terror, pushing and punching, frantic to save myself, insane with anger at those in my way. Warmth spread down my legs; I realized I had wet my pants. An instant later, I was knocked sprawling from the truck, and landed heavily, face-first on the hard ground.

Its guns blazing upward, an armored vehicle rumbled past, spewing me with dust. I rolled away to where a number of infantrymen, all kneeling, fired their rifles again and again at the planes. The aircraft, which were quite small and clumsy looking, streaked away, then made long, looping turns.

"Here they come again!" a soldier wearing a mask of dirt yelled. He turned to me and in a confidential tone, as though he were telling me a secret, repeated, "Here they come."

The Russian aircraft—I counted four of them—were diving at us with their guns blazing. I aimed my rifle skyward, excited at the prospect of firing at the enemy. I pulled the trigger. To my astonishment, nothing happened.

"You've got the safety on, idiot!" someone sneered.

By the time I had fumbled the safety off, the planes,

one of them trailing smoke, had already zipped past and were now headed away. The battle, as quickly as it had begun, was over.

I was so filled with disappointment at not having gotten off a single shot that it was a long moment before I turned my attention to the destruction the planes had left in their wake. A peculiar silence had settled over everything; even the cries of men in pain sounded muted and unreal. I stood up, and realized my legs were shaking. I turned in a circle, then leaned against a tree to keep from falling. Numbly, I stared. A small fire had broken out in some brush across the way. One wounded man was crawling away from it; others lay unmoving, singly and in clusters. Most of the trucks were scattered alongside the road, many of them damaged. One truck was continuing on alone, rolling slowly away down the sloping road. Driverless, fully engulfed in flames, its burning tires going round and round like huge pinwheels, it continued on. Nearing the bottom of the hill, it turned on its own, flopped onto its side, then all but disintegrated in a single, monstrous explosion.

"That was really something, wasn't it!" a soldier near me whooped excitedly.

"Yes," I said in a monotone, then wandered off amidst other survivors, feeling very strange and confused.

Medics were taking care of the seriously injured, while those with minor wounds just sat in a daze, waiting their turn. I noticed one boy sitting beside the road, blood from a gashed scalp making it appear as though he were wearing a bright red wig. He was looking around. His eyes met mine, and I made my way to him.

"My name is Erik," I told him, not sure why I was introducing myself.

"Hals Kessler," he said pleasantly, not sounding at all pained or concerned about his wound.

"This is going to hurt a bit, Hals," I said, continuing to wonder at my oddly professional and authoritative tone. I gripped the splinter. I yanked, and a bit of metal about the size of a pencil stub slid free easily. "A little souvenir for you, Hals," I said superciliously, handing him the bloody splinter.

After bandaging Hals's head, I wandered off, feeling very self-satisfied, as if I were some great doctor who had just completed a very complicated bit of surgery. Glass crunched underfoot. I found myself headed down the road, examining bits of burning debris and oversize red pancakes of dirt and blood. Surprising me, a veteran shoved a spade into my hands.

"Get to work." He gestured with his head toward a shallow ravine a short distance from the road.

Spade in hand, I made my way to where a detail of soldiers was working about the lip of the ravine, shoveling dirt onto a bloody jumble of bodies on the bottom. Among them was a boy I had known only as Rosy Cheeks.

Stupid Children

Three trucks had been lost in the air attack. Eleven soldiers had been killed, nine of them conscripts.

"Stupid children. Never even got a chance to fire their rifles."

The words, spoken long ago—by the seemingly deranged man on the troop train—kept going round and round in my head, as did images of Rosy Cheeks and the other boys, now underground, tangled together in death.

There were fewer wounded than it had seemed at first, less than twenty, but seven of these were serious. Shortly after getting underway again, we entered Ovruck, a town where a medical station had been set up in a church. The truck carrying the seven badly injured soldiers pulled off the road and stopped in front of the small church-turned-hospital. As our convoy continued on, headed away from the place, I looked back; I saw something I will never forget. A nurse wearing a blood-smeared rubber apron was making her way toward a smoke-belching incinerator. In her arms was a human leg.

Because of the losses we sustained in the air attack, platoons were reorganized. At his request, Hals Kessler joined ours, the Seventh, and sat next to me on the truck as the convoy wound its way eastward. Head wrapped turban-style with bandaging, he repeatedly thanked me for coming to help him out after he had been wounded. The way he made it sound, I was the greatest person in the world and he owed his life to me.

Though all of Hals's praise and gratitude were undeserved, the two of us soon became fast friends. Jakob and Oskar made it a foursome. As the convoy growled along, Hals worked with the point of his field knife to make a hole in the piece of shrapnel I had removed from his head, then used a boot lace to hang the thing around his neck. He wore it until the day he died.

Our next taste of battle came a few hours after leaving Ovruck, and the church-hospital there. A rocket, fired from a *Panzerfaust,* a bazooka-like weapon, hissed past, no more than a meter above the truck in front of us in the convoy.

Fifty-caliber machine guns erupted all along the convoy, and from the trucks we began firing our Mausers as well. A breathtaking barrage pounded at a cluster of trees in a field off to our right. Again and again I pulled the trig-

ger of my rifle. The trees were shredded by gunfire—as
was a man, a partisan, who had been hiding in them. Hit
by countless bullets, he did a wild death dance; it was
comically hideous, and despite myself, I laughed—
ashamed, embarrassed, and puzzled by my strange, inap-
propriate reaction. Two other figures were suddenly racing
across the field. One carried a *Panzerfaust*; the other, a
child of about eight or nine, lugged a shell for the weapon.
Almost instantly, they met the same fate as the first man,
and fell heavily together under the barrage we laid down
on them.

"Cease fire!" Dobelmann yelled.

The smell of burned gunpowder and cordite was redo-
lent in the air. The Mauser was hot in my hand. I checked
the breech, to make sure the action was clear. I reloaded,
wondering if any of my shots had hit anyone.

"That was just a kid that we killed," intoned Oskar.

"A kid that was trying to kill you," said Dobelmann,
his horrid face half-turned toward us.

Our ultimate destination was battalion headquarters at
Tarnapol. Our first glimpse of the place came at night and
when we were still some twenty-five kilometers from it.
Suddenly ahead, and far to the east, there was a series of
false sunrises. What we were seeing was a distant artillery
barrage. First came multicolored flashes of light; then
faint rumbling sounds, like rolling peals of thunder, fol-

lowed. Nervous eyes, hooded by helmets, exchanged glances. I held my Mauser tightly. Though the night was cool, my hands were sweating terribly. I felt like I was wearing wet gloves.

Later that night we reached a supply dump in a densely wooded area. The place, under heavy guard, consisted of hundreds of boxes stacked to different heights, and looked like a scale model of a small city. Dobelmann ordered us off the truck, and then began talking with a master sergeant, a tough-looking little man who seemed to be in charge of the place.

"Gilburt," said Dobelmann. "You do not recognize me, do you?"

"Rolf!" said the man, peering closer in the dark. "Is that you?"

"Yes—what a grenade made of me." The two began talking about old times, the master sergeant keeping his eyes averted from Dobelmann's face.

In a shack, lit by a single yellow-glaring kerosene lamp, I could see men, soldiers. One was sound asleep, curled up in a corner; another was trying to read something by the yellow light; most just sat, their arms clasped around their legs and their heads resting on their knees. One of them looked up; his glance seemed to fix on me. I looked away.

More of the trucks from our convoy arrived at the supply dump, most of them piled high with munitions. Our drivers joined those in the shed. Some of the trucks were already fully loaded with supplies; others, just vacated by us, were relatively empty. On orders from Dobelmann and other *Felds,* we loaded all the trucks with as many crates as they could carry. Some of the crates contained food, clothing, and medical supplies. Most contained munitions—bullets, mortars, mines, and artillery shells—and weighed a ton.

As soon as a truck was completely loaded, the master sergeant called out a name, and a soldier emerged from the yellow glow of the shed. Their expressions varying from grim to terrified, they climbed behind the wheel and drove off, headed for various units of the Fourth Division in and around Tarnapol.

I talked to one of the drivers as he awaited his turn to leave. I do not remember his name. His voice quavering with nerves, he told me that he and the other drivers were from a "punishment brigade." Men in such units, for some infraction of the rules, were denied leave and mail from home, ate last, and were given the most hazardous duty. In this case, they were being made to drive trucks containing large amounts of explosives, often almost straight through enemy lines. No more than half of them were expected to make it.

We finished up at about three in the morning. All of the trucks had departed. We undid our bedrolls, lay down wherever we could, and soon fell into an exhausted sleep.

Mules

The next thing I knew, I was being nudged awake. It was still dark out. I strained to see the dial of my school watch. It was a little after four A.M.

Shivering in the early-morning cold, we ate hard biscuits and drank tepid ersatz coffee. Dobelmann called the platoon together. We joined in a loose circle around him, looking like a congregation of new converts kneeling with their minister.

Battalion headquarters at Tarnapol was still some eighteen kilometers away, he told us. We would be lugging in supplies to headquarters, basically coming in the back way. En route, we would pass through the ruins of the town of Vinnitsa. Under relentless artillery bombardment, our troops were holding the town to keep the road open—and thus our supply line to battalion headquarters.

"It is essential," said Dobelmann, "that you and the supplies get through." He looked around at us. "Any questions?"

None were asked.

Each of us was given roughly twenty-two kilograms to stow in our packs—mostly wax-wrapped, five-cartridge packages of ammunition. Combined with the rest of our gear, all told, we carried almost seventy pounds each on our backs.

"Move out," said Dobelmann.

As we headed off from the supply dump, then down long slopes through forests of pine, I was struck with an odd notion. All around me were soldiers, rifles in hand. I had the strange feeling that I was being escorted by bodyguards, that the sole purpose of all the others was to protect me.

It was midmorning when we reached a crossroads, the remains of Vinnitsa all around. Bent beneath the weight of our heavy packs, in loose columns, we made our way down what was left of the main street of town. From the ruins, grimy, desolate-looking German soldiers watched us with blank gazes. Blasted-out cellars had been turned into makeshift bunkers sprouting machine guns. On the roof of a ruined theater, snipers and spotters lay spread-eagled, scanning the outlying fields through binoculars and telescopic-rifle sights. With my gaze turned upward on them, I almost walked headlong into a trolley car—rusting, off its tracks, and with layers of sandbags on the roof. As I skirted it, from within came hushed voices speaking in German. They stopped. A face appeared in a window. Briefly, disinterested eyes met mine; then the face disappeared.

Most of Vinnitsa had been reduced to long piles of rubble. A few structures remained standing, though many of these were little more than shells. Vividly, I remember one two-story place. Most of the front had been sheared off, leaving a clear view into the somewhat intact interior. It reminded me of home; the lower floor had been a shop of some kind, the upper story had been the living quarters. A red-and-white checkered curtain in an upstairs room fluttered in the breeze.

"Auf Wiedersehen!"

Next door to the place, two soldiers sat at the foot of a stairway that went nowhere. One called out "good-bye" in German, and then gave us a mocking little wave. The other, using a finger as a make-believe knife, made a slashing motion across his throat.

Soon, we were headed up a long slope, leaving Vinnitsa behind. It began to rain. Gentle spray turned into a downpour. A cold wind gusted. *Gummimäntels,* rubberized shawls, were pulled from packs. Heads lowered to heavy, drifting sheets of rain, we trudged on.

We finally reached the crest. Our platoon rested briefly. Then we were on our way again—long, broken queues of us, slogging along a road that wound around through low, barren mountains. Rain danced on helmets and *Gummimäntels.* Sodden clothing clung to our bodies. Boots were thick with mud.

I didn't think I could make it. By the weight of the pack, I was being crushed—downward and forward. Often, when the grade got especially steep, I leaned far forward. I felt like a mule with a dead man on its back.

Once I stopped for only a couple of seconds, struggling to catch my wind. Dobelmann screamed in my ear: "Get moving!" He lowered his voice. "The faster you go, the sooner this will be over."

"Danke, Feldwebel."

I thanked Dobelmann. I straightened my back and kept going.

Perhaps an hour later, trucks began passing us. Gradually, out of the fog and rain, a network of bunkers came into view, as did veterans, many of them gathered in clusters under dripping awnings of canvas and corrugated iron. Eyeing us suspiciously, they watched our approach, then motioned us forward with their weapons.

"Battalion headquarters," someone behind me said.

I looked around at a labyrinth of interconnected trenches, bunkers, and artillery emplacements, including tanks that had been backed into sandbagged niches. Other than their long cannons, they were all but invisible. The same was true of the bunkers. Dug into the hillside itself, only stout timbers and sandbags marked their presence.

A man a few steps ahead of me stopped. He turned around. I found myself almost face-to-face with Dobelmann.

"Seventh Platoon," he barked into the rain.

Jakob, Oskar, Hals, and others from our platoon appeared beside me. Dobelmann conferred with another

Feldwebel. A few moments later, he led us splashing along through deep trenches, up to our ankles in water and muck. He stopped and aimed a dripping hand at the entrance to a bunker. "We are going to have to break up the platoon, at least temporarily. The first five of you, in there. The rest of you, follow me."

Eager to get out of the rain, I followed Oskar, Jakob, and two other boys onto a low platform of rough-hewn timbers, then pushed past a canvas sheet covering the entrance.

"Ah, so what have we here!" a voice exclaimed light-heartedly from the semidarkness as we filed into the bunker.

With the others, I moved tentatively ahead, half blind in the dim light, enshrouded in warm, stale air that reeked of cabbage and unwashed bodies. As my eyes adjusted, the interior of the surprisingly large bunker came into focus.

Two junior officers engaged in a game of chess scarcely looked up, but grimy men lounging in bunks and gathered around a combination furnace and stove were eyeing us. All had matching, sneering grins on their faces. Our presence, as we stood there unsure of what to do, seemed to amuse and disgust them at the same time.

"Karl," said one, "our reinforcements have arrived!"

"Ah, then we are saved!" came the reply.

A man in filthy long underwear sauntered toward us. Mouth bulging with a great lump of chewing tobacco, he stopped in front of me. Scowling, he looked me up and down with dark, slanted eyes. His round face was dirty and bristling with an uneven stubble of black beard, and his teeth were covered with green and brown scum.

"All the men are dead," he said, gazing contemptuously at us. "Now they are sending us boys." He spat a gob of tobacco juice, and then shaking his head, wandered away.

The Welcoming Party

The bunker was one large, long room. The ceiling was of wood slats, the walls of sandbags and heavy beams, and the floor of hard-packed earth. Much of the space was taken up by wooden bunk beds, odds and ends of other furniture, and a potbellied stove. An arrangement of tin cans connected together formed a stovepipe, which disappeared up through a hole in the ceiling. Rainwater constantly dribbled down the thing, and there was a pair of muddy pools on the floor. Wet clothing hung everywhere—from the corner posts of bunks and from lines that had been strung up.

There were five of us "reinforcements," as we were referred to, in the place. Hals, to my disappointment, was not among our group. I knew Jakob and Oskar well; muscle-bound Meyer Fassnacht was among our group, as was a chirpy, undersize soldier named Willi.

"Your luncheon is ready," a fat soldier in a filthy apron announced, his tone mockingly ceremonious.

We piled our packs near a ceiling support beam. Then,

still in our wet clothes, we lined up with our mess kits near where a large kettle bubbled pungently on the stove.

"I hope what I have made is to your liking," the fat man said, as he and another man doled out bread and tea, then ladled soup into our bowls. "You look as though you have had a hard time of it, a long, hard walk in the rain." He laughed. "Have you had a long, hard walk, boys?"

No one answered him. Continuing to wonder at the strange way we were being treated—at the contempt the veterans had for us—we sat down at a greasy wooden table and began eating in silence. The tea was weak, without flavor; the bread was ersatz—made of flour mixed with sawdust—and was difficult to swallow; but the soup—of cabbage, carrot tops, and chunks of meat—was thick and good. Ravenous, I downed it all within short order, as did the others, and we were pleased when we were offered more. Even the tea, weak though it was, at least was hot; and the bread, though it tasted like soggy wood, was still filling.

"There's one!" a wild-haired man suddenly shouted.

His excited call captured the attention of all the veterans in the bunker, except the two officers wrapped up in their chess game. Armed with bayonets, clubs, and sharpened sticks, the motley bunch descended on a corner at the back of the place. Wondering what all the commotion was about, we made our way to where they were gathered.

"There's a whole nest of 'em in there I tell you," the wild-haired man chortled. He was on his knees, aiming the beam of a flashlight through gaps in the wall of sandbags.

"Ya, I think I see them!" A big-nosed man began jabbing away with a long stick.

"What's in there?" Jakob asked.

"Rats," replied a rather soft-spoken soldier. "The walls are crawling with them. Killing rats—that is our mission in life in this stinking hellhole."

"Good source of protein," said our cook. "And tasty!" he laughed.

It took a moment for what he had just told us to sink in. My eyes met those of Jakob, Meyer, Oskar, and Willi. Together we looked to the pot of soup and then to our near-empty mess tins on the greasy table.

"Meat is in short supply," said the cook, a wry grin on his face. "So we have to make do as best we can."

"I like rat meat," I said, not wanting him to get the better of me. I fought off a sudden wave of nausea. "I've had it on a number of occasions."

"I have, too," said tall, lanky Oskar, his voice feeble and unconvincing. He started to say something else, then bolted from the bunker as the veterans laughed. Over the sound of their laughter—and of the rain—we could hear him retching outside.

The rat hunters howled, the cook loudest of all. Finally, snickering and wiping dumb grins from their faces, they returned to the attack. All business now, and very excited, the bunch of them began scurrying about along the wall, trying to peer behind it, now and then jabbing away with their various weapons.

"You in there, you filthy beasts?" a huge, hulking man screamed at the wall. "Well, if you are, this'll kill ya!" He swallowed air, pressed his open mouth to a space between two support beams, and discharged a loud and long-lasting belch.

"There it goes!" yelled another man, and immediately there was a flurry of wild jabbings and thrustings with various sharp instruments at the back wall of the bunker. Over the laughing and cursing there suddenly came a series of wretched squeals from behind the wall, and when the weapons were withdrawn they were covered with blood and gore. The men tried to extract the dead rat by yanking on its long, naked tail. But finding that the creature was too large to be pulled through the narrow gap, with great delight they commenced hacking it to bits and removing its corpse piece by piece.

Another attack was then quickly launched in another part of the bunker.

Sopping wet, Oskar returned.

"Sorry," he said.

"For what?" I said.

Jakob patted him on the back.

Cold, tired, and disgusted, the bunch of us began to idle about, wondering what we were supposed to do with ourselves.

"Sir," I said, taking it upon myself to approach one of the chess-playing junior officers, "where would you like us to put our gear?"

"Take any one of the empty bunks," he replied without looking up from the game.

"You will not be here long anyway," said his chess partner.

Wondering what this comment meant, I put my pack at the foot of one of the bunks, then sat down and began removing my muddy boots.

"Hey, not *that* bunk!" The man in filthy long underwear was coming toward me with a bloody bayonet. "That's Lindemann's bunk! What are you taking his for?"

"Sorry," I said, getting up. "I didn't know it belonged to someone else."

For some reason, my response was greeted with snickering laughter, and a moment later the five of us newcomers found ourselves surrounded by rat hunters.

"What made you think you had the right to take Lindemann's bunk?" the wild-haired man demanded.

The man in the filthy long underwear moved to within an inch of my nose. He shifted the bulge of chewing tobacco from one cheek to the other. "Taking Lindemann's bunk was a real low-down thing to do, *Dummkopf*!" he said, filling my nostrils with his reeking breath, grinning all the while.

I stood looking at the man, not knowing what to say. That I and the other newcomers were being goaded and toyed with was more than obvious. But what was the big joke? What exactly was all this nonsense about? Uneasy, surrounded by this smirking, bullying bunch, the five of us were at a loss as to what to do.

"Which bunks should we take, then?" Jakob asked, his voice cracking with nerves.

"Well," said a man scratching at a boil on his neck, "you can take Erhardt's or Ritter's or Klopp's. Or I guess it really wouldn't matter if you took Lindemann's."

"I don't understand," said Jakob.

"They're all dead." Mr. Long-Underwear squirted a jet of brown tobacco juice from a gap between his scum-coated teeth. "What is there to understand about that? Ritter, Klopp, Gruber, Pedersen, Erhardt, and Stroebel—they're dead. Lindemann, too."

"We have enough bunks for all of you," a little man with vacant eyes said dolefully.

"Gone to a better place," said Mr. Long-Underwear, "as we all will for our Führer!" He clicked his heels together as his right arm shot forward in stiff salute. "*Heil* Hitler!"

One of the junior officers looked over at him with an absently disapproving look, then returned to his game.

Mr. Long-Underwear put a grimy hand on my shoulder. "Lindemann got it yesterday, or was it the day before?" He turned to his comrades for an answer.

"The day before," replied the wild-haired one.

"Was he your friend?" I asked.

"Haven't got any. It is unwise to have friends, because they have a bad habit of getting killed. In some fashion or the other, everyone meets with an unfortunate accident." He suddenly cocked his head to listen. At first there was only a delicate humming somewhere above, then the sound swelled to a monstrous drone. The bunker convulsed as a deafening crash drowned out every other sound. Jakob, Fassnacht, and Willi scuttled under tables, chairs, and bunks. Terrified, Oskar and I grabbed hold of a swaying support beam. I stared at the ceiling; sand trickled down from the gaps between planks. Black smoke poured in through a lookout slit at the front of the bunker, and chess pieces and cutlery danced off tables and clattered to the floor.

"Almost a direct hit," said Mr. Long-Underwear matter-of-factly.

Neither he nor any of the other veterans had bothered to take cover, with the exception of the sad-eyed little man. Shaking with fear, he was curled in a ball near Jakob's feet, hugging himself and making a strange whining sound. The chess players were scrabbling around for kings and queens and rooks and pawns, bemoaning the destruction of their game.

"Let's see, where was I?" mused Mr. Long-Underwear, sitting down on a footlocker and looking up at me. "Ah, yes, we were discussing the departure of Private Lindemann from this earth. It was quite an ugly death," he said, raising his voice over the sound of a heavy detonation somewhere in the distance. "They say he was found pinned to the bottom of a trench by a seventy-six-millimeter shell. The bomb fin, I'm told, protruded from his back like a ventilator. Went right through his back and chest and then into the ground, but didn't explode."

"But even so, it killed him," the fat cook added with black humor.

"He was here only a matter of hours," said the wild-haired man. "He was lucky. Lucky Lindemann—he got to die quickly!" He gestured toward the bed where I had been sitting. "Go ahead, take his bunk. Who knows, maybe you'll be lucky, too!"

Prisoners

Early the next morning we were put to work repairing damage done by the rain and artillery fire. Trenches had collapsed and some were half filled with muck and water.

Though it was foggy, I had a much clearer picture than the day before of where we were. The bunkers were near the top and center of a horseshoe-shaped range of hills, the slopes of which were a fortress of trenches and heavy-artillery emplacements. Below was more of the same. Stretching far off into the distance was a muddy flatland of zigzagging trenches, redoubts, blockhouses, and tank traps. Beyond that lay empty flatland with nothing but black veins of charcoal. Though I could see nothing of them, the Russians, I heard it said, were encamped some-where to the northeast, and their numbers were growing daily.

Hals was in the same work detail with Jakob, Oskar, and me; we were glad to be with our friend again. Dobel-mann and other *Feldwebels* were in charge of us, directing us as we toiled away on the grubby, backbreaking chore.

We scooped bucketfuls of brown water from the trenches, restacked sandbags that had fallen, and filled more bags—gunnysacks—with mud. We were soon sopping wet and filthy. Of the *Felds,* only Dobelmann got his hands dirty, so to speak, and actually helped with the work.

Later that afternoon, caked with mud, bone weary, my hands lumpy with blisters, I returned to our bunker. Having worked more than nine hours, I wanted nothing more than to crawl into my bunk and sleep. I was cleaning up as best I could when a major's adjutant pushed in through the canvas-draped doorway to the place. Stripped down to an undershirt, pants, and boots, I snapped to attention—as did everyone, including the rat hunters, seeming as though they'd suddenly been transformed into real soldiers. The adjutant, to my surprise, called out my name. I stepped forward and saluted.

"Prisoners were taken last night during a probe, Private Brandt," said the adjutant, a well-groomed, handsome man who reeked of cologne. "You will come with me, please."

He did not even wait for me to get into uniform. I pulled on a heavy sweater from home, and then hurrying to catch up, followed the man and his scent up a well-traveled path. Over the brow of a hill, we passed row after row of tanks, then approached what appeared to be a huge pigpen enclosed by barbed wire. Inside were twenty or thirty Russian soldiers. Nearby, under a canvas awning, at a crude desk made of boards propped up on boxes, sat a stoop-shouldered little corporal and a lieutenant with thick glasses. Magnified eyes looked me up and down as I was handed a list.

"You will ask these questions—in Russian—then translate the responses for me," the corporal ordered.

The bespectacled lieutenant yelled to the guards, telling them to "bring out the monkeys."

The guards began hustling prisoners out from the barbed-wire enclosure. All the Russians were barefooted, and though it was bitterly cold, most were shirtless. None had identity tags, such as those we German soldiers wore; instead, they carried papers, which they turned over to the corporal.

"How many men are in your division? How many tanks? How well are your troops fed? Are your gasoline supplies sufficient? When is the offensive on our position to be launched?"

Over and over I asked these and other questions in Russian, then translated the answers into German. The corporal took careful notes. If a prisoner refused—or even hesitated—to answer, either the lieutenant or adjutant put a gun to his head. The last question, that concerning an anticipated Russian offensive, was the most important. But none of the prisoners—all ordinary foot soldiers—knew when it was to begin. Even with a gun pointed at them, the most precise answer any gave was "soon."

The prisoners were a dismal, wretched-looking bunch. I remember only two of them at all. One was a skinny man who had been hit in the left elbow, and whose bare arm

looked like a bent red stick. He asked for medical attention. When I translated, the lieutenant laughed. The other
Russian I remember most was a tough-looking character
who, after being interrogated, glanced at me and, under his
breath, hissed *"abarot!"* Russian for "traitor." Apparently
he had concluded that I was a Russian who had sold out to
the enemy—not only because I spoke the language fluently but also because I was out of uniform.

After the interrogation, the prisoners were led off under heavy guard toward a wooded area. I asked the
cologne-reeking adjutant what was going to be done with
them.

"They will be digging latrines," he replied, a tiny
smirk on his face.

The corporal belly-laughed.

It was not latrines the prisoners would be digging.

The Front

The following afternoon our platoon was ordered down to front-line trenches. Hals, Jakob, Oskar, and the rest of us followed Dobelmann down one of the steep, crisscrossing trails leading from the bunkers and artillery emplacements on the hill. Rifles in hand, lugging full packs, we made our way across the flatlands toward our most forward line of defenses—a vast, semicircular maze of interconnecting open trenches. Beyond was a blackened wasteland of rolling hills. It had once been a forest; the blasted remains of a few trees still sprouted from the sooty ground. Strung between these were coils of barbed wire.

We relieved the Fifth Platoon. The soldiers—mostly young reinforcements, like us—were a dirty, weary, and miserable-looking bunch. When Dobelmann informed them that they were being relieved and sent to the rear, up to the fortified bunkers behind us on the hill, they were overjoyed.

Smiling, they scrambled out of the trenches.

Scared, we scrambled in.

Four feet wide and four feet deep, the almost shoulder-high trenches were muddy, littered with trash of every sort, and stank of urine and rotting garbage. All around, the soil was cratered and plowed looking, as though an insane farmer had tilled his land into a mindless pattern of furrows. Only boots, burned cloth, and chunks of metal grew from them.

"A Russian assault is probably imminent."

Dobelmann gathered us together.

"An attack could come at any time. It may be just a probe, or it may be an all-out assault." Steel blue eyes in the disfigured face scrutinized us. "They cannot go around us or outflank us. To our right flank is swampland; to our left is the river, the Pript. Our artillery atop the hill behind you gives us command of the surrounding land. The Ivans must take the hill, and to do so they must first come through our front lines—through *you*. They will try to—"

Momentarily silencing Dobelmann—and startling all of us—Mr. Long-Underwear and two other veterans dropped feet-first into the trench. More followed. They were all business. They laid stick grenades in neat rows on the sandbags fronting the trench. Machine guns were set up on tripod stands. We watched as the one nearest us was loaded by locking down a heavy, glistening belt of ammunition into the breech. Metal boxes filled with more ammunition were placed within easy reach, as were wooden boxes containing flares and grenades. With a bay-onet, a moon-faced man pried off the lid of a long box then removed a tubelike weapon. Dobelmann asked for the thing.

"How familiar are you with the use of a *Panzerfaust*?" asked Dobelmann, cradling the heavy weapon.

Only the muscular Meyer Fassnacht and a boy with a gold-capped front tooth had ever fired one before, Dobel-mann quickly discovered. The scars on his face turned to angry red lines. "Didn't they teach you *anything* in train-ing camp?" he demanded.

Oskar's Adam's Apple bobbed up and down. "No, sir. At least not much. I was in camp only three weeks. Our *Obergefreiter* said we'd learn soon enough all we needed to know once we got to the front."

Dobelmann waited a moment before beginning to speak again. He patted the hollow metal tube. "The *Pan-zerfaust* is a rocket launcher, primarily an antitank weapon," he began, then continued, explaining how it was operated as it was passed from hand to hand.

"What else—if anything—did they teach you?" asked our platoon leader.

A platter-faced boy spoke up. "How to clean, load, and fire a rifle." He smiled faintly. "And how to prepare and throw a grenade."

"First you unscrew the safety cap," said Jakob, inter-rupting and trying to show that he knew as much as Platter Face. "Then you count to three, pull out the red button, and then give it a toss!"

"Incredible!" muttered Dobelmann.

"Thank you," said Jakob, mistaking this for a compliment.

"*Nein, mein Knabe!* No, son, what I mean is that it is 'incredible' that they are not only sending children into this slaughterhouse, this abattoir, they have not really trained you—at all." He picked up a stick grenade, removed the safety cap, then pointed to an exposed button-like projection. "Look, young man," he said to all of us, but directing his gaze at Jakob. "You wait a three-count after pulling out the *button,* not after unscrewing the cap."

"Yes, *Feldwebel,*" Jakob stammered, his face turning red with embarrassment.

Dobelmann continued with his impromptu lesson. He went over the use of flares, machine guns, bayonets, and then mines.

"Crank the plunger counterclockwise," he said, indicating a box from which wires trailed out into the scarred, black earth beyond our trench. "Lift the plunger. Give it a quarter-turn clockwise, then push it down." He pointed at shell craters about a hundred meters off. "When the Ivans come, they will jump into the shell holes which we have packed with detonation cord, dynamite, and S-4 mines. When they jump in, blow them back out—in pieces."

"'In pieces'?" said Hals, his voice a breathy whisper.

Tense eyes, shaded by the lip of a helmet, were locked on Dobelmann.

"It is either you or them, *Knabe*. You are fighting for your lives and for those of your *Kameraden*."

He paused. A silence settled over our group in the trench, and again he looked from face to face. My stomach clenched in a knot as Dobelmann's gaze came to a rest on me—then on my rifle, a standard-issue four-cartridge Mauser. He took it from my hands and held it up.

"Always take good care of your weapon," he said. "Treat it with the respect, care, and gentleness you would a lady. Treat your weapon well, and it will treat you well." He handed the rifle back to me, and then crossing his arms over his chest, looked me in the eye. "But what's your best and most important weapon, boys?" he asked.

The question was directed at me, and I was supposed to answer it, I felt. "I don't know, *Feldwebel*," I said, wiping hands wet with nerves on my pants, and hanging my head. I felt stupid, as though I had failed an important test.

Dobelmann pointed at his head. "Your most important weapon is your brain—your mind power. Things may get very rough—far more so than you think possible. When that happens, and you're so scared you think you are going to lose your mind—don't! Do not lose control. If you do— if you permit that to happen—then you will be dead." He scowled. "I hope you are paying very close attention to what I am saying. Are you?"

"Ja, Feldwebel," we answered in unison.

"Remember—always, always, always keep your wits about you." He wiped away perspiration that had collected in a webwork of scars beneath one eye. "If heavy shelling should start, just keep down. Think about nothing but what is coming next and what you must do to be ready for it."

Ready for what? I wanted to ask, but nothing came out.

"When the shelling is over, that is when the tanks and infantry come. Fire everything you've got—and keep firing. *Panzerfausts* at the tanks. Mortars, mines, and *fausts* will disable or destroy some—maybe most—coming your way. But if tanks start breaking through, do *not* panic. You can run laterally through the trenches, and you can belly-crawl backwards, but never—*never*—get up and try to run away. If you get up, you are dead. You've got a better chance of surviving by just staying in your trench and letting the tanks pass over. Your rifles and grenades—use those on the infantry. Bring down all you can. But the time may come when there is really no more that you can do. And if the Russians have breached our lines and are all around, and you have no chance of escaping, just play dead." He smiled crookedly. "Play dead ... but keep thinking." Strong blue eyes blinked inside a mask of horrors. "Good luck, gentlemen," he said, coming out of a crouch. "Hopefully, the Ivans will not come at us on our shift. But if they do, be ready." After assigning us all different tasks, he left us. On some mission known only to himself, he headed away down the trench, past ever-growing numbers of our troops.

That evening a kitchen truck brought us hot rations. As we ate, Jakob and Willi began talking about Dobelmann. Not only had we all come to look up to him, there was something very mysterious about the man. Long-Underwear, who had been listening idly to us, leaning back against the trench wall and smoking a cigarette, turned his head our way. Listlessly, he blew a stream of blue-gray smoke at us.

"Rolf Dobelmann was a philosophy teacher and gymnastics instructor," said Long-Underwear. "He's married and has three kids. After a grenade went off almost in his face, and after months in a hospital, he had a friend write a letter home that he was dead. He was too ashamed of how he looked to go home. He reenlisted. The war took everything from him. The war, now, is all he has left."

From ten p.m. to one a.m. I was posted with two veterans as forward lookouts about half a kilometer beyond our lines. Each of us had a flare gun, and we were told to fire a blue flare if we saw any large-scale movement. We saw nothing.

After our relief showed up, we made our way back to our lines, through the endless labyrinth of open trenches. I crawled into our trench, pulled a blanket over myself, and immediately fell asleep.

I'm not really sure when the artillery barrage began. It was a couple of hours before dawn, I think. At first it did nothing but annoy me. All I wanted to do was sleep, but that quickly became impossible.

I sat up and looked around.

I saw a long, open trench full of scared faces. The closest was Jakob's. His mouth was open, and the explosions made his teeth flash red, like little neon signs going on and off. Hals was stuffing packets of bullets into the multiple pockets of his cartridge belt. Across from me, skinny Oskar was a stiff silhouette. He looked like a pole with a helmet balanced on it.

At first, most of the rounds were landing far behind us, blasting away at our heavily fortified bunkers on the hillsides. There was a lull; then suddenly I heard a sound like a freight train coming directly at us. I lay flat in the bottom of the trench. There was a huge flash, then the bottom of the trench bounced up into me. Dirt and debris rained down. Shrapnel whizzed past. More freight-train-like shells hurtled through the night. I curled into a ball in the trench as the whole world seemed to detonate.

"Stop it!" Jakob screamed.

As if in response, the shelling suddenly ended.

"It's over," mumbled Hals. "Is it over?"

Warily, we rose up. I looked into the black, cold maw

of night, then behind me at a landscape dotted with what looked like hundreds of little campfires, all started by the shelling.

"My hand hurts," said Willi.

"Oh," I said.

Willi held up his arm. It was only a stump.

"Medic!" Jakob screamed.

A Souvenir

Dawn came as a backlit, silver shroud of fog.

In the bombardment of the night before, many areas of our trenchworks had collapsed. Wretched and dirty, we repaired the damage and rebuilt the trenches as well as we were able. A horse-drawn cart, carrying those who had been killed during the night, rattled past. Fortunately, we had none to add to the five or six blanket-wrapped bundles in the wagon. Willi had been our only casualty of the night.

We ate when we could. I found some crackers in my pack and shared them with the others.

I remember Hals cutting an apple with a bayonet and giving a wedge to Jakob, Oskar, Fassnacht, and me. I remember chewing as I looked around at the vast network of trenches and gun emplacements that made up our front lines, fog rendering it all grainy and surreal. I remember Dobelmann and another veteran pulling a damp tarpaulin off a machine gun. I do not remember the shrieking whines that in-coming shells make; I have no memory of the sound of artillery, nor any of the blast that knocked me right out of the trench.

I was brought back to consciousness by explosions, screams, and a rain of hot mud. My mouth tasted of blood and apple, and everything around me was coming apart. Someone grabbed hold of me and was pulling me by the arms. I couldn't see who it was; everything was out of focus, including the person trying to help me. I cried out in pain; my shoulders felt as though they were being ripped out of their sockets as I was dragged back to the trench—and then pulled face-first into it.

The bombardment continued. I just lay on my side in the trench. The shelling tapered off. Only as it came to an end did I really start to come to my senses. I forced myself to a sitting position, with my back to the wall of the trench. I realized Hals was beside me, and wondered why he was just sitting there like that. I was surprised when he leaned over and put his head on my shoulder.

"What are you doing?" I asked, feeling confused and irritated.

He said nothing; he just continued to rest his head against me. It was then I noticed the warmth, the wetness. Blood was spilling from a gash in his deeply dented helmet. His eyes were blank, dotted with mud.

I put my arms around him. I sobbed. I screamed his name, shaking him, trying to shake him back to life.

A strong hand had grabbed hold of my shirt. Dobelmann pulled me around to stare him in the face.

A Souvenir

"There's no time for that, boy!"

I cursed him.

He patted my shoulder and he shoved Hals's rifle into my hands. A moment later I was at the lip of the trench, between Oskar and a bearded veteran. I felt nothing—only the tears drying on my cheeks. In my hands was the Mauser, resting in a crevice between two sandbags and pointed into rolling morning fog.

"Hals is dead."

"I know," replied Oskar, his voice a lifeless monotone.

I realized that artillery was still being fired, but now it was coming from *our* side, from the heavy artillery emplacements on the hill behind us.

"We're shelling them," said Oskar

"But they're not shelling us," I added.

"That's because they're coming now!" hissed Dobelmann.

Feuern!

I looked back at Hals, then again forward. A heavy, hot bead of sweat spilled down my temple. Gripping my rifle, my finger on the trigger, I stared into a blinding fog.

An eerie quiet settled over everything.

I became aware of a distant squealing, from somewhere deep in the haze.

"Tanks," I said to Oskar.

"Infantry first," said Dobelmann. "They will throw infantry at us first."

From our lines, green flares were fired, turning the fog an odd chartreuse color. The flares had been a signal to our mortar crews. Projectiles were dropped backward down hollow tubes; the tubes coughed them back out—as far as seven hundred meters. Rendered invisible by speed and fog, the high-arcing projectiles seemed simply to disappear, then heavy *kruumphs* sounded somewhere deep in the haze.

The mortars stopped firing briefly.

"Hold your fire!" Dobelmann growled at us.

Feuern!

All along our lines, helmets gleamed darkly, wetly. Our trenches bristled with weapons, pointed at the screen of fog. Coming from somewhere in it was the sound of hundreds of fast, heavy footfalls. Men in boots running; gear rattling; panting.

Getting louder.

Getting closer.

At two hundred meters, Russians burst screaming out of the fog.

"Feuern!" Dobelmann yelled for us to open fire.

Our lines erupted. Again and again, I pulled the trigger, fired at oncoming brown uniforms, reloaded, kept firing. Adding to the horror of sound, all along our lines, mortars, light artillery, and machine guns blasted at the Russians. More and more brown uniforms crumpled, went down. Still, endless numbers kept coming. Some stepped on land mines; they and those around them disintegrated. Mortar and artillery rounds scissored others. At a hundred meters, many were snared by barbed wire. They struggled to get free of the stuff, twisting and turning in every direction.

One . . . two . . . three . . . four.

I counted my shots as I fired the semiautomatic Mauser in my hands at men entangled helplessly in barbed wire.

Bullets.

At first I did not know where they were coming from. They peppered the ground around me, kicked fans of dirt in my face. They pinged off metal, ricocheted off the concrete blockhouse to my left. The air whined with them. They thumped against sandbags, and they tore through flesh.

A veteran to my right screamed. He grabbed his face; blood spilled through his fingers. Putting an end to his agony, a bullet hole suddenly appeared in his helmet, and he dropped to the bottom of the trench, dead.

"Bastards!" I screamed.

I saw gun flashes coming from in front of us, from Russians hiding behind whatever little cover the land provided, and hiding behind their own dead.

I fired, trying to hit men moving about in a crouch. I aimed, fired four shots, then fumbled shells out of my cartridge belt, spilling many as I reloaded, then aimed again. Looking down my gun sight, I saw men draped with barbed wire. I took careful aim; I fired. A fifty-caliber in the blockhouse hammered them.

A human form slithered into a shell crater and joined a group of steel helmets collecting there, not eighty meters away. A Russian machine gun appeared on the lip of the crater.

"When the Ivans come, they will jump into the shell holes. They're packed with detonation cord, dynamite, and S-4 mines." Dobelmann's words going round and round in my head, I searched for the detonator box, only to find it already in Jakob's dirty hands. Eyes wide, he gave the

plunger a quarter turn, then shoved it down. Not one, but an entire network, of craters erupted.

"Did you see that?" Jakob yelled, seeming both startled and pleased by what he had just done.

More craters in that wasteland exploded.

Then there was just the chatter of machine-gun fire coming from our lines, and occasional pops and bangs of rifle fire. Scattered groups of Russians were running away beneath a drifting ceiling of smoke and fog. Some of the fleeing brown uniforms went down, hit in the back. I realized I was seeing all of this through one eye: My left eye was closed; with my right, I was looking down the hot barrel of my rifle. But I was not firing.

I could not shoot anymore.

I lowered my Mauser.

Numb, I watched as the last few Russians limped away. Some made it, some did not.

It's over, I thought. "Thank God."

"Cease fire!" Someone yelled.

A few more pops of rifle fire from our lines.

Then there was only silence. My ears were so used to the blathering of battle that the quiet was startling. I stared. The fog was breaking up, dissolving. I looked out at yellow sunshine bathing the ground below. In many places, it was carpeted with the dead, lit an ethereal gold-yellow for a moment by a combination of fog and sun. I remembered a scene painted on an interior wall of a chapel in Vilsburg. It was a religious painting, but I knew little else about it. A beautiful girl—an angel, perhaps— was hovering in the sky, above the earth. That painting, which I might never see again, was spread before me. It was in my mind, and I was looking out at it even as I was looking out into a well-lit reality of the most horrible kind: shattered ground; bodies everywhere.

I suddenly felt sick; my legs began to tremble. I sat down on a fallen sandbag in the trench, and found myself looking at Hals again—at his mud-spattered eyes. His mouth was slightly open, as though he were about to say something. Hanging from a bootlace around his neck was a piece of shrapnel.

"A little souvenir for you, Hals," I heard my own voice saying in my head. The words seemed to be coming from the past, from long ago.

Tanks

As a young boy back in Vilsburg, I had been in only one fistfight—with a boy named Gus. Why we fought, I really can't remember. Before the fight, I had been filled with anger—then fear. During the fight, adrenaline had raced through my body, filling me with strength; when it was over, I was so drained I could hardly move.

That is how I felt after the attack—only incredibly more so. I was rubbery-legged, shaky, and struggling to catch my breath. My ears rang; my jaw and head ached from being thrown out of the trench; and though I had not noticed it before, a bullet had grazed my lower left arm; my sleeve and hand were wet with blood.

I wanted someone to bandage the wound, which had begun to throb. I wanted to clean up, and perhaps get something to eat. Then take a good, long rest.

The battle was over, and we had won. Certainly no more would be expected of me.

These were the thoughts that were passing through my

mind when I suddenly realized the fight was not over; it had only begun.

"Now they will be hitting us hard," said Dobelmann.

I wondered what he was talking about.

"Check your ammunition!"

I felt in my bullet pouch. Only a few cartridges remained. As others were doing, I grabbed bullets from an ammunition box and refilled my cartridge belt. I was reloading the Mauser when I became aware of a distant squealing. Off in the black, undulating field ahead, tanks loomed into view—seeming to rise up from the bowels of the earth.

"Mein Gott im Himmel!" mumbled Oskar. "Dear God in heaven!"

A sudden quiet settled over our lines. All that could be heard was the horrid squeal of the tanks. Russian infantrymen jogged behind, many in a half-crouch.

"A full, frontal assault," whispered a veteran, his voice full of terror.

I looked from him to Oskar. His scared eyes met mine.

"Hold your fire!" Dobelmann ordered, an edge of fear to his voice, a *Panzerfaust* in hand. "Wait till they're in range."

German heavy artillery, far behind us on the hill, began firing—and continued nonstop. Our light artillery and mortars joined in. Red explosions flowered everywhere amidst the tanks and infantry. Adding to the incredible blathering of noise, the Russians were answering back with their own long-range ordnance—the shells seeming to come from nowhere, from miles away. Tank cannons flashed at us. The ground vibrated with detonations. Part of our trench collapsed. I fell. I heard screams. I saw a boot with a foot in it.

I was looking up into red, black-rimmed eyes as Oskar pulled me back to my feet. He was saying something, but I did not know what.

A chorus of defiant, fearsome yells was coming from the Russian infantry. Thousands of men, it seemed. They were running. And the tanks—I was horrified at how fast they were coming. Sheer terror made my whole body feel cement-hard. It was difficult to move, even to breathe. I heard a cry; I looked over my shoulder.

A tourniquet was around Fassnacht's leg. He was looking at the boot with his foot in it, and crying in pain and cursing as someone dragged him away by the arms.

The tanks grew closer. Ugly green, with a red star.

"Feuern!" Dobelmann yelled.

Like a shooting gallery. From all along our lines came crackling pops from rifles. And then the staccato rattle of machine guns.

Green tanks. Brown uniforms. I aimed at the men, firing as fast as I could. Just shooting. Not knowing if I was hitting any of them. Most kept coming. I felt like I was firing blanks.

"I can't stop them!" I screamed.

A moment later I found myself heaving grenades. I

was amidst a group, all of us doing the same. We kept tossing grenades as fast as we could, as far as we could. Like kids throwing rocks.

A tank's cannon was turning in our direction. I stood frozen, awaiting its blast. Instead, coming from behind me, a sizzling hiss passed my ear. The tank lifted up on its treads and made a gonglike noise. It ruptured from within, blew apart like a tin box.

I looked at Dobelmann, a smoking *Panzerfaust* on his shoulder.

Bullets peppered all around me.

Out of a chaos of smoke and erupting soil, more tanks emerged. Pitching and bucking crazily, they bore down on us, ripping through wire entanglements and rolling over the bodies of their own dead and wounded. One tank was knocked off course by a mortar round, but then it was moving again—directly at us, and wobbling. Another spilled its treads, and came limping to a stop. It began to burn; a crewman, his clothes in flames, ran out of the wreckage and right into the path of another tank. I saw men thrown into the air. A broken, life-size rag doll of a body landed on the turret of a tank. It was as if it had been dropped from heaven. With the body still on its turret, the tank's twin machine guns hammered us.

All along our lines, men dropped.

"My God!" screamed Oskar. *"Mein Gott!"*

Off to my right, I glimpsed a tank speed past, through our lines and right over the trench there.

"Oskar! No!"

He had thrown his rifle down and was fleeing, as were others. Oskar, like a skinny horse on just its rear legs, was galloping awkwardly away. He and another man were punched in the back at the same time and sent sprawling by the tank's machine guns. Oskar struggled to his feet, only to go down again, battered by another spray of bullets.

"Fix bayonets!" someone yelled.

My bayonet dangled in its scabbard from my belt; there was no time to attempt to slide it into the lock on the barrel of my rifle. Russian soldiers were already leaping into the trench, and all about me was a frenzy of hand-to-hand combat. I fired my rifle point-blank into the shirt of a soldier; at the same moment, I felt something jab my arm from behind. Squealing in pain and abject horror, using my rifle as a club, I slammed it down on the helmet of a Russian.

"No!" he cried in Russian. *Nyet Pazhalusta!*

I was looking at his face. I couldn't shoot him. I turned and ran; a slippery smear of flesh and gore in the trench sent me flying. I landed in a heap. Rising to my knees, someone slammed into me, knocking me sideways onto corpses and debris. I saw Germans running. I struggled to my feet. Something speared my right knee. I screamed in agony. I fell against the back wall of the trench. I stared in frozen horror. A mammoth tank—dragging great, long strands of barbed wire with it—churned out from clouds of smoke and dust. It rose up on the sandbagged front edge of the trench—one of its huge iron treads clawing at air—the other broken, unrolling. For a moment it stood suspended above me. I dove for the ground, screaming, as the thing's massive underbelly came down at me.

Behind Enemy Lines

Iron smashed into my head.

I was lying on my back when I came to. I had no idea as to how much time had passed. My entire skull pulsed with pain, and I was nauseous and dizzy. My right knee throbbed. It was dark, and for a moment I thought it was night. I turned my head and saw daylight, and from somewhere heard Russian being yelled. I looked up, and again saw the underbelly of a tank, about two meters above me; one tread was broken, putting it out of action. It had come to a stop above me, straddling the trench. I ran a hand through my hair. It was wet with blood, and there was a large lump just above the hairline. I reached down and felt my pounding right knee; it was bloody, and my fingers came upon a jagged piece of shrapnel that felt embedded in the joint. I rolled sideways. All around me were the ugly leftovers of the battle: shell casings, wooden boxes, helmets, weapons, empty canisters—and dead soldiers, both Russian and German. More of the same filled the trench to either side of the tank.

When I turned to look, a dead arm flopped down on the back of my neck, knocking my head downward. My chin came to rest on the gray-green of a dead German's chest. And looking right into my face was another face, that of a blond Russian boy, his lifeless eyes locked open in disbelief. I looked away as I suddenly became aware of the sound of distant battle—then almost jumped at the sound of a nearby gunshot.

I heard someone pleading in German—then another shot. I belly-crawled a half meter and peered out. What I saw sickened and terrified me. A Russian officer was methodically seeking out the German wounded and shooting them. A lumbering oaf of a foot soldier, using a bayonet, was dispatching other Germans. He seemed to be enjoying what he was doing. And many of those he was bayoneting looked already dead; he was just making sure.

I froze at the sound of nearby voices.

"I want this tank operational immediately!" someone was demanding in Russian.

"I will do my best, master sergeant," came the response. "Parts are in short supply."

"Just get it done!"

The voices were close, but I could not tell from where they were coming exactly. Two booted legs jumped into the trench, followed by another pair. My heart pounded so hard and loud I was sure it would be heard. Two Russians knelt down in the trench beside the tank and examined the dangling, shattered tread. Remembering Dobelmann's words, I played dead among the dead.

"And how does the idiot think we are supposed to repair it?" groused one of the men.

"We will need another T-34 tank to pull it free," came the reply.

"Prinisitye mnye pazhalusta adin T-34!"

Both laughed. One had joked that their superior officer acted as though they could repair the tank by magic.

The two figures rose, and out of a slitted eye I saw two pairs of legs headed away, down the trench. They paused for a moment and huddled with a man who had the white cross of a medic on his helmet, and helped him tend to a badly wounded Russian soldier. Between the three of them, using a blanket as a makeshift stretcher, they trundled the wounded man out of the trench.

Entangled in carnage and debris, boxed in by the walls of the trench and the bottom of the tank, I lay there wondering what to do, too frightened to do anything. I wanted someone to help me, to talk to me, as my mother would, and tell me what to do. I looked for help, and saw only the dead.

From somewhere down the trench came another bang. Perhaps another wounded German had been executed?

My gut knotted with fear. Over and over, I kept hearing what Dobelmann had said to us just one day before.

I tried to think.

We had been overrun. In the distance, in the direction of the bunkered hill, fierce fighting continued; battles that I could not see were being fought. More Russians were passing by every minute. I heard them; I saw them scramble through the trench.

I was trapped behind enemy lines.

If discovered, I would be killed. Even playing dead would not save me; even dead, once found, I would be skewered on the end of a bayonet.

I had only one chance, I knew, to save myself.

The dead eyes of the blond Russian boy seemed to be watching me. With my fingers, I closed the lids. Strange though it may seem, I did not want him looking at me and at what I was about to do. In that cramped and bloody charnel house beneath the tank, I removed my clothes— even my socks and underwear—then exchanged my clothes for his. The task was very difficult. I was in considerable pain, especially from my right knee, from which the ragged bit of metal was protruding, and it was extremely awkward undressing then trying to re-dress the inert body, the limbs of which were already turning stiff.

During this last part of the gruesome process, I had to stop. The two Russians I had heard before returned; they crawled in amidst the bodies and examined the tank's underside, then commenced cutting and pulling out long strands of barbed wire that had become entangled in its drive wheels. At this juncture, I was no more than half done re-dressing the corpse in my own uniform. Sick with fear, only a few centimeters from the two men, I lay frozen in place, certain that I would be found out. But the minds of the two—both seemingly mechanics—were on other things; they paid not the slightest bit of attention to me, to the half-dressed corpse, or to any of the bodies.

Finally, they left, and I finished my ugly chore as fast as I could. In the pocket of the brown jacket I felt a bulge, and removed a wallet. In it there were a few rubles and a military identification card. In the dim light I tried to make out the name. I was unable to, and returned the wallet to my pocket.

I crawled. I pulled myself from under the tank and along the trench, over more bodies and more trash. From somewhere came the sound of approaching vehicles and far-off voices. Russian voices. Amidst more dead and more trash, I leaned back against the wall of the trench, thinking back. Hals had been killed, and before that, Willi had lost an arm, Fassnacht a foot. Oskar had been shot in the back, running away. But Jakob was still alive, as far as I knew, and so was Dobelmann. I looked at the faces of the dead in the trench, wondering if I would see Dobelmann or Jakob—and hoping I wouldn't, hoping that somehow they were still alive.

Sitting there leaning against the wall of the trench, every part of me hurt, especially my knee. I pulled up the brown pant leg. The knee was badly swollen, and just below the kneecap a piece of steel was protruding. It looked as though a large, misshapen nail had been driven into my leg. Something occurred to me: The shrapnel had hit my knee before I had changed uniforms, so there was no tear in the pants; someone seeing this might become suspicious. Rubbing the woolen fabric back and forth over the jagged spike, I ripped a hole in the pant leg, exposing the wound.

Over trash, dead bodies, and collapsed earth, I crawled out of the trench. Not knowing where I was going or what I was doing, I found myself wandering along what had been our front lines, limping, using a Russian rifle for support. The dead were everywhere, in whatever final pose death had forced upon them. Gutted tanks and other vehicles continued burning. I became aware that I was approaching a man—a Russian—sitting against the charred and shattered stump of a tree. His face was caked with grime and his hair singed off. He held badly burned arms out in front of him. They were lathered with some kind of yellowish unguent, as though they had been frosted. He was grimacing in pain; brown eyes gave me a distressed, curious look.

"Galava krushitsa." I told him in Russian that I was very dizzy.

Brown eyes blinked, looked at me uncomprehendingly as I hobbled past him. The pain in my knee became more than I could bear. I sat down on a broken slab of concrete. Before me, amidst heaps of other debris, was what remained of a shattered German blockhouse. One wall had been shorn away; and inside the place I could see dead men and a broken-looking weapon, a light artillery piece. An uprooted tree lay beside the blockhouse; beneath its fallen branches—a bouquet of dead, black-brown sticks— lay the body of a German officer. His body looked broken everywhere; his uniform was smoldering.

"*Moy!*"

"*Nyet, moy!*"

Across the way, two Russians were arguing like a couple of kids. Scrounging for souvenirs, food, and any usable goods, they had come upon something they both wanted for some reason. They started bargaining, haggling: for a can of peaches, one would give the other a German sheath knife. I grabbed to where my sheath knife should have been, and realized there was none: I was wearing a Russian uniform and Russian gear, and there was a canteen there instead of a knife.

From far behind me came a sudden flurry of gunfire, and then a series of explosions. Reduced to a spectator, I turned and looked to the horseshoe-shaped hillside—German battalion headquarters. A huge Soviet flag—red, with a hammer and sickle—had been raised. It looked tiny in the distance, but it told me most of what I needed to know. Flurries of fighting were still going on in various areas of the hill, in and around the bunkers. To the south, German tanks were burning; a few others were in retreat, firing as they raced backward. Clearly the battle had been lost.

We had been defeated.

I didn't know if I even cared.

I cared about the friends I had lost. Hals and Oskar. Their deaths filled me with grief. And I was angry with them—for dying, for leaving me.

I turned my attention to my knee and began pulling at the spike of shrapnel buried in my flesh. I could move it a little from side to side but couldn't pull it out, I leaned back against the blockhouse, my eyes on the dead German officer.

I heard footsteps, and looked up to see a large number of fresh Russian troops coming in my direction. I was terrified, momentarily; it was my delusion that they were coming just to get me. Frightened, I stood up. Using the wall of the battered blockhouse for support, I made my way around to the other side of it—as though I could hide there; then I did an even stranger thing: I waved at the Russians, as I had so many years ago at parading *Wehrmacht* troops.

Surprisingly, someone waved back.

Leaning heavily against the Russian rifle, I heard a scratching, rustling sound on the other side of the blockhouse. I saw a hand—a left hand—come around the other side of it. The hand was in a claw shape; fingertips dug into loose soil. A man, the German officer I had left for dead on the other side of the blockhouse, pulled himself into view. His face covered with grime and soot, his legs seemingly useless, he was dragging himself along the ground like some sort of fire-blackened, badly injured alligator.

He looked up at me, and at first I didn't realize that what he was seeing was the enemy—and perhaps his executioner.

"Nein!" he rasped.

I did not see the pistol in his right hand until he fired. A bullet whined past my face. He fired again. I flew backward as something hot hit me in the side; then I was just sitting on the ground, pressing a hand to my belly and looking at the German. He was continuing to slither away. A rifle shot rang out. He slumped, stopped moving.

"Pamagite!"

A Russian soldier hurried toward me, a smoking rifle in hand, and he was calling for others to come help him.

Strong hands helped me lie down on my back.

A bearded face loomed into view. "Are you hit bad?" the man asked in Russian.

I looked up and saw what I thought was my grandfather.

"Dyshyte narmal'na!" Breathe normally, he said. Kneeling beside me, he pressed a pad of gauze to the wound in my side. "Just take it easy, son," he said in Russian. "You're going to make it."

Part Two

Charade

On a stretcher, two Russian soldiers trundled me across the ripped-up terrain. My leg hurt terribly and the wound in my gut burned and made me sick to my stomach; still, I was alert. I was put onto a horse-drawn cart. Already seated in the thing was an oddball congregation of four look-alikes. They gave the appearance of a bunch of mummies; the heads, chests, and arms of all of them were wrapped in gauze bandaging. All had suffered burns of a similar nature, perhaps at the same time and place, and apparently they were from the same unit. They seemed to know each other well and were jabbering away in Russian. They complained of the pain from their burns; but at the same time they seemed rather pleased to be together and also somewhat amused by the similarity of their appearance.

I was vaguely curious about what had happened to them, but said nothing. I was in too much pain and too scared to really care.

"You have a water bottle," said someone behind me.

I didn't realize he was talking to me, or remember that there was a canteen attached to the belt of the uniform I was wearing.

"You going to drink that?"

I felt a tap on the shoulder. I turned, then looked up. Blue eyes were gazing down at me out of round holes in a head mask of white bandage. A white-gloved finger pointed at the canteen.

"The flash burns," said a bandage-encircled mouth. "They're making me near dying of thirst."

"Take all you'd like," I said in Russian.

"Spasiba, syn," he said, thanking me.

The canteen was unhitched from my belt and passed around. Empty, it was returned to me. There were more mumbled thank-yous from the group of mummies as an unconscious man with a shrapnel wound to the chest was loaded aboard the cart.

"You from the Luga line—the Luga Operating Group?" asked a mummy across from me.

Fear welled up inside me. I didn't know how to answer; I did not even know what the question meant. *It's best not to remember anything,* I told myself. *And say as little as possible.* Desperately, I tried to think of the Russian word for amnesia, but, ironically, I could not remember it, and found myself staring blankly at the odd group. There was puzzlement in their eyes.

"What's your name?" the same man asked.

"I don't know," I said meekly, a sudden wrenching pain in my gut causing me to grimace. I put my hand to my bandage-capped head. "I'm trying, but I can't!"

"Poteria pamiaty," said the mummy across from me, using the Russian term for amnesia. He nodded in understanding.

"I don't know who I am!" I told him with half-feigned terror.

He glanced around at his look-alikes. "Join the group," he said with a pained, raspy laugh. "We're not sure who we are, either!"

I lay in the cart for what seemed like an extremely long time, feeling sick, light-headed, and as though I was being cooked by a hot morning sun. I remember other wounded men being loaded on and someone telling me I was losing a lot of blood. But I have no recollection of the cart ever moving.

My next memory is of being on a bus, which surprised me greatly. The seats had been removed, and instead there were wooden bunks filled with patients. The thing was old and battered and rocked every which way. A nauseating pain clutched at my belly and I was wet with perspiration. An IV needle was in my arm, a rubber tube connecting it to a bottle of plasma overhead. My abdomen, head, and right knee had been freshly bandaged. My leg was in some kind of splint, and putting my hand to my knee I found that the spike of shrapnel had been removed.

"Why are we going to Kolesk?" a man in a bunk across the way kept muttering in Russian. "I do not live in Kolesk. I want to go home to Smolensk!"

A medic with haggard eyes and wearing a stained white apron gave the man a shot to shut him up. I am not sure, but I am fairly certain he gave me one as well. Regardless, when I next awoke, I was no longer moving, and I felt very little pain. However, only with great difficulty was I able to open my eyes. It felt like they were glued shut. Blinking, wiping bits of crust from my lashes, I was surprised to find myself in a schoolroom, the wooden walls an ugly green and many of the windows broken and boarded up. It was afternoon, and the few unbroken windows gleamed orange. I saw maps on the walls, a portable blackboard with a jagged crack down the middle, and books stacked in a corner. But there were no desks. Instead of desks, the place was filled with hospital beds and wounded men and boys. Groggily, I tried to sit up.

"Ah! Welcome back to the world!" said a pleasant voice in Russian.

I had been looking to my right. Turning to the left, my eyes met those of a middle-aged man in a bed next to a *pyech,* a coal-burning furnace. The man's head was shaved, his complexion waxy and sallow, and from the waist down his body and both legs were in a cast. Despite his appearance and condition, he had a friendly, almost happy expression on his face.

"I think you are going to make it," he said in a joking tone. "*Are* you going to make it?"

I blinked. I looked at the man but said nothing. I was confused, disoriented; fear gripped me, and I wondered how I had ended up in the strange place. All around me were people—patients—speaking Russian. I closed my eyes. I drifted on the edge of sleep. I dreamed. I began to reawaken. Dreams became memories—of real things, awful things. I rolled sideways.

"He's coming around," said someone.

My eyes were still closed, but I was awake. Thinking. I needed time to think. What had happened to me? I tried to make sense of it all. And where was I now, and what should I do?

"I'll be back," said a female voice.

I was in a Russian hospital of some kind, I knew. I'd fallen into a trap, one of my own making. And I was terrified, worried. A charade; I would now have to become what I appeared to be, just another wounded Russian soldier—one who had trouble remembering much of anything.

But how long and how well could I pull it off?

I spoke Russian, of course. But how well? Would some trace of an accent, some misuse of idiomatic expression, some flaw in my pattern of speaking give me away? And then, too, there was the fact that I knew very little about Russian life and culture; I only knew what my grandparents had taught me, most of which was about Odessa, their birthplace and where they had grown up.

I would have to be cautious, alert. I would have to listen carefully and learn quickly and well.

My life depended on it.

Across the room, something fell with a clattering bang.

I opened my eyes.

"Ah, coming back to the world again, are you?" said the man in the body cast next to me.

I took a deep breath. Nervously, I looked around the schoolroom hospital, then at the man, the huge cast on him making it appear as though he was wearing cement pants.

"I am Nikolai Mikhailovich," he told me.

Forgetting myself, I almost responded in German. But I caught myself in time.

"Zdrastvuite." I said hello in Russian, my voice little more than a dry croak. I desperately wanted a drink of water and looked around hopefully for a nurse or someone who might bring me some. I saw no one in the place but patients.

"How do you feel?" Nikolai asked.

I worked up a bit of saliva and ran my tongue around inside my parched mouth. "Thirsty," I rasped. *"Mnye khochitsa pit!"*

"Someone will be by sooner or later," he told me. "They are very busy. They have so many of us to take care of, and more keep arriving each day."

90

I closed my eyes again and felt greatly relieved. I had said very little, only a few words. Still, I had communicated without seeming to have aroused any suspicion. I took a deep breath. My head ached; I became aware of a feeling of pressure, as though someone were squeezing my skull. I put a hand to my head and found that it was tightly bandaged. I blinked, then rolled my eyes upward, trying to see the skullcap of heavy gauze I was wearing.

A doctor with wild-looking, curly white hair was hurrying past. I raised my hand, like a schoolboy trying to get attention. The doctor never noticed me. He kept right on going. A patient across the room called out to him, but even that did not slow the doctor. He rushed from the room and disappeared down a hallway.

"They are very busy, like I said," Nikolai mused.

I lay back and again tested my Russian. "I am so thirsty," I mumbled.

I have water," said a voice behind me. "Take some."

Looking over my shoulder, I realized for the first time another bed was right behind mine, and I caught a glimpse of the back of a man's head and a tin cup extended toward me in a bandaged hand.

"Spasiba," I said, thanking the man and taking the cup.

"Do not drink much," said the man. "You've been gut-shot, like me. You drink too much too fast you'll hurt so bad you'll wish you were dead."

I thanked him again, then took a sip. I wanted to drink

the whole thing, but Nikolai took the cup from me and handed it back to the other man.

"How long have I been here?" I asked Nikolai.

He made a face as he thought back. Like a caterpillar arching its back, a bushy eyebrow went up in thought. "Three days now, I think."

"Three days!"

"They operated on you—" Again the eyebrow went up. "They operated on you the first morning after you got here."

"Operated on me?" For a moment I was sure the man was lying or teasing me. How could so much time have passed and so much have been done to me without my knowing it? Feeling under the coarse sheet, then lifting it up, I had more surprises: My right leg was in a cast, my abdomen was tightly bandaged, and coming out of the bandage was a red rubber tube. Leaning over the side of the bed, I found that the tube trailed away down to a jar on the floor. It was partly filled with a pinkish liquid. "What is this thing?" I asked, sickened by the sight of the tube stuck in my belly. "And what is that stuff coming out of me?"

The man behind me answered. "I have two of them in me. The doctors put tubes in after surgery to drain out any blood or fluid that builds up in your gut. Mine come out in a few days, and then they are going to stitch up the holes in me."

"Oh," I said.

"You've got a through-and-through. Bullet went in your side and out your back."

I lifted up the sheet again and took another look at myself, then lay back, feeling weak and tired. I closed my eyes. An instant later a rush of nervous fear hit me.

"What is your name, my friend?" The voice was Nikolai's, and his head was turned toward me.

I remembered to say what I was supposed to say. "I don't know," I said, my head wrinkling with the real worry and confusion I felt.

"Zabivchivost?" he said with a laugh, using a Russian word meaning to forget some ordinary, everyday bit of information. He seemed to think I was joking.

I explained that my head wound had left me unable to remember anything, that I was suffering from amnesia— *poteria pamiaty.* Then I lay back, feeling suddenly very scared. "I'm crazy," I said. "I don't have any idea who I am." I hoped I sounded as convincing as I did anguished.

Nikolai apologized for laughing at me—not once, but several times, as though he had committed some great sin. *"Da,* it must be a very troubling feeling not to know who you are."

I nodded.

"Well, how are you doing?" said a nurse, a pretty blond girl, her skin so white it looked transparent. She put a hand to my head, and reaching into a pocketed apron took out a thermometer. "Open your mouth, Aleksandr."

"What?" I blurted.

"Ah, so at least we know your name!" exclaimed Nikolai.

Confused, I looked at the nurse. "Why do you call me Aleksandr?"

Flustered, she studied a clipboarded chart at the foot of my bed. "Aleksandr Dukhanov," she said, her voice whispery soft. "Serial number K487944. Two Hundred Twentieth Armored Division. That is what your identity papers say." She blushed bright pink. "Is there some problem?"

I just stared.

"The boy did not remember his name—until now," said Nikolai by way of explanation.

"Amnesia," said the man in the bed behind me.

"Ah, I see," said the nurse. She smiled faintly at me. "We have had others with *poteria pamiaty.* Usually the memory comes back." She slipped the thermometer under my tongue, then pressed her fingers to my wrist to take my pulse. "Let us hope that yours does, too, Aleksandr."

Aleksandr. Aleksandr Dukhanov. That was the name of the dead boy beneath the tank, the boy whose uniform and papers I had taken. And now I was him.

"Little by little it will come back to you."

Speechless, I stared at her, unable to tell her I already remembered everything—who I was, what had happened to me, and what I had done, both before and after the battle. All the awful details. I wanted to scream. I wanted to yell out the truth. But I couldn't. I was afraid. It was so strange, so twisted: I was caught in the middle of a lie, pretending to be unable to remember things I wished I could forget.

"X"

The man behind me was named Mikhos. Next to him was Boris, who had been badly cut up by shrapnel. From them, and from Nikolai in the bed next to mine, I learned that I was in the village of Alreni, about forty kilometers or so from Tarnapol, in a schoolhouse that had been converted into a hospital. The place had five rooms. Three were used as wards, one as a kitchen and dispensary, and the last as an operating room.

My terror at being found out continued to gnaw at me, though no one seemed the least bit suspicious. I did make one small mistake, but even this went almost unnoticed. I told Boris that my knee was pounding; instead of the word for knee—*kalyena*—I said *bidro,* which means "hip."

Boris asked if I had been wounded in the hip, as well.

"Nyet," I told him no, struggling to keep the nerves out of my voice. "But I must have twisted it or hurt it a bit somehow."

He nodded.

As the days passed, I settled into the hospital routine.

Breakfast was around seven. For me, because of my abdominal wound, this usually consisted of bread, tea, and *schi,* cabbage soup. For the others there was always fresh fruit from nearby orchards, *myshtsas,* a type of muffin, and sometimes *yaytsa v smyatku,* soft-boiled eggs and sausage. But even before breakfast was served, there were countless other tasks that had to be attended to by the nurses, orderlies, and other staff members. The converted classroom rang out with calls from the men.

"Nurse, please, a shot for the pain!"

"Hey you—comrade, water! Please, I am going to die of thirst!"

"Please, somebody, a bedpan!"

The last of these was the most common morning call. And orderlies would hurry to the men and bring *German helmets* for them to relieve themselves in. Probably collected after some previous battle, the helmets were what were used as bedpans. Using them for this bothered me at first, but after a while I got used to it and hardly gave it a thought.

The staff worked endless hours trying to take care of the hundred or so patients in the place. They usually looked haggard and totally exhausted from the never-ending chores that had to be done—changing our dressings, and feeding, bathing, and cleaning up after us. They also had to get recovering patients up out of bed and back on their feet. As far as the military was concerned, the idea was to send these men back to the front; but being short-handed at the hospital, the doctors kept many on as long as possible to help out.

The hospital had only two doctors—Dr. Swaroff, the man with the bushy white hair I had seen on my first day, and Dr. Rostovick, a nervous little man whose eyes always looked frozen wide with anxiety. We saw very little of our doctors—or of the skilled nurses. From dawn to dusk—and sometimes far into the night—they were in the operating room doing surgery. Taking care of the patients in the ward was left mostly to male orderlies and volunteer nurses from the village of Alreni, few of whom had any real medical training.

In charge of the ward staff was Zoya, a stocky woman with a booming growl of a voice. Katerina, the blond nurse with the alabaster skin, was Zoya's niece. She wasn't at all like her aunt; slender and delicate, she spoke so softly it was often hard to make out what she was saying. Lina, also blond, was a tireless worker and very efficient, despite the fact that she was so short she had to drag around a box to stand on when working at the beside of a patient. Marusia was a somewhat dull-witted and clumsy girl who always seemed to be making a mess of things; but because she had a beautiful face and figure, almost all the men seemed to be in love with her. Tamara, the youngest of the unskilled nurses, had long, brown hair that reached almost to her waist, dark, mysterious eyes, and a gentle smile. She lived with Zoya and Katerina.

Rubin was the head orderly. He was easygoing and

well liked by the patients and the rest of the staff—except Zoya, who always seemed to be finding fault with him. Vlad and Oleg, half brothers, and both as big and strong as bears, were the only male orderlies who worked at the hospital on a permanent basis. The rest were recovering patients. We also had a single guard for the hospital—Sergo. With a dented, surgically scarred forehead, Sergo was a former patient—and so badly brain-damaged he had been declared unfit for military service, but had taken it upon himself to play soldier guarding the hospital.

During a German offensive, Alreni had been attacked and briefly occupied. Most of the inhabitants had fled eastward, abandoning the town. A deathlike stillness seemed to hang over the place. The window near my bed framed a stretch of dreary-looking wood houses and buildings, and beyond that a pine-forested mountainside. Directly across the way were a stable, an abandoned dry-goods shop, and an extremely small house with a green door that forever hung cockeyed on its hinges. Often, in the roadway between the schoolhouse-hospital and these buildings, I would see our guard, Sergo. By himself, rifle on his shoulder, he either stood at attention or marched back and forth.

Other than to groan, feel miserable, and sleep, there was little for us to do to pass the time except talk. Mostly, the patients talked about their homes and families, about the work they had done before the war, and about things that had happened to them on the battlefield—especially about how they had been wounded. Nikolai, in his plaster pants, had been wounded in both legs when his battalion had accidentally been bombarded by their own troops using "Stalin organs," multiple rocket-launchers. Mikhos had been shot twice in the stomach trying to get to a wounded comrade. Boris had been a few meters from a soldier who had stepped on a mine. The other soldier had been killed; Boris, though badly injured by the blast, had somehow managed to make his way on his own to an aid station several kilometers to the rear.

My story was probably the strangest of all—but, of course, I could not tell it. I could only lie and say I had trouble remembering anything. The others started guessing where I was from, which made me nervous. In Russia there are dozens of ethnic groups, and countless languages and dialects are spoken. Because of my blond hair, blue eyes, and manner of speaking, it was the consensus that I was either from Silesia or Odessa. I did nothing to dispel this conclusion and thanked them for trying to help.

With everything locked up inside me, I thought constantly of home—of my mother and grandparents—and of Hals and Oskar, and of Jakob, Willi, Fassnacht, and Dobelmann. And then there was the soldier—Aleksandr—whose uniform I had taken. I said as little as possible and mostly just lay looking up at a ceiling of white, peeling paint. It looked like dead, flaking skin.

Every part of me hurt, and I was so scared and lonely and lost that I often felt like crying.

"X"

If it hadn't been for Nikolai, I don't think I would have made it. Nikolai, who had a wife and two young sons back home, was to me like the father I had never known. He talked to me a lot and always had a smile and an encouraging word for me. Another thing I received from him was a new name. I hated being called Aleksandr or Alex, and told him so. He began calling me X.

"It suits you," he said.

I agreed.

The Visit

Now and then there would be a death in the ward. The body would be tagged then trundled away on a wheeled cart—which, with gallows humor, was referred to as the happy wagon. One of those taken away in the thing was a soldier whose bed was across the aisle from mine. He had suffered severe head and leg wounds, and had never regained consciousness after being brought to the hospital.

One afternoon he began making an odd rowing motion with his arms. For hours, he kept it up. It was very strange, almost as though, unconscious, he was rowing away, off into another world—the next world. He rowed far into the night.

The next morning he was gone.

And another man—very strong and muscular looking—was in the bed. At first I did not know what to make of the new man. He looked so healthy and fit, and I was at a complete loss as to what might be wrong with him; then gradually I began to realize that he was not moving—at all. He was paralyzed from the neck down. Lying flat on his back, he stared at the ceiling. Only once did he turn his head in my direction. I said hello to him. He didn't answer, and his gaze went back to the ceiling. He blinked, and a tear—one he could not wipe away—slowly trailed down the side of his face.

Nurses, orderlies, and other patients sometimes tried to talk to him. Only rarely would he respond, and then only with one- or two-word answers. He was all alone with his misery, and wanted to keep it that way.

I felt a strange bond with this man. He was keeping everything locked up inside. Like me, for his own reasons, he did not want to—or could not—talk about what he was dealing with inside. Explaining what he was thinking and feeling was impossible. And there was no one to whom he could turn for help.

One morning there was a sudden flurry of activity, and through word of mouth I learned that the little schoolhouse hospital was going to be inspected that afternoon.

"They look for malingerers, soldiers shirking duty by pretending not to be well enough yet to fight," Nikolai told me. "They also look for impostors, anyone not qualified to be in one of their wonderful military hospitals. And they check the staff, to rate their performance, and so forth." Nikolai lowered his voice to nearly a whisper. "They are a bunch of pompous asses. Communist bigwigs—stupid, self-important bureaucrats."

Fear swept through me; Nikolai's words went around and around in my head: *"They also look for impostors."*

Certainly, I fit the description!

So far, no one seemed to have noticed that I was different, that I was German. I had spoken little, and very carefully; even my mannerisms were very Russian—the way I shrugged, for example. So far, none of the staff or patients seemed to have detected anything unusual about me. But would I withstand the scrutiny of the inspectors—government "bigwigs," as Nikolai had put it, people actively seeking someone such as me?

A horrid fantasy played in my head. In it, Communists were pointing at me as I lay in bed, yelling at me, exposing me as a German. "But I am half Russian!" I would cry. "I am as much Russian as I am German!" Laughing, they would beat me to death with their fists.

"Is something wrong?" Nikolai's head was turned in my direction.

I realized I was gripping my bedding with both hands, and sweat had broken out on my brow.

"Are you all right?"

"Da," I said. "Just a cramp in the belly."

He nodded.

I wiped my brow, tried to relax. I looked out at the ward.

In preparation for the visit, the staff was scurrying around, working even harder than usual to get everything in top shape. Even our doctors, Swaroff and Rostovick, made a relatively rare appearance. Rostovick was even more nervous than usual, and buzzed around like a windup toy, his words coming out mechanically fast as he ordered people around. Swaroff, too, seemed a bit edgy. But it was the orderlies who seemed the most worried of all. One of them, a man named Yuri, even asked Rostovick if he could get into an unoccupied bed and pretend he was a patient.

"Nyet!" screeched Rostovick. "Definitely not!"

Yuri disappeared briefly. When he returned he had a bloody bandage—that he had probably taken from the trash—wrapped around his head.

Swaroff told him to take it off. Yuri did as he was told.

"Why are the doctors and orderlies so scared?" I asked Nikolai, trying to hide my own terror.

"If the doctors are found wanting, they may be sent to the front—to triage stations, which are far bloodier and more dangerous than here." His brow furrowed. "I know, I was in such a place for two days. As for the orderlies, if the inspectors decide that any of them are well enough, they will be sent back to fight—and probably die."

As it turned out, the officials did not make their visit until two days later. Lina, standing on her box, had just finished changing the dressings on my wounds and was emptying the jar of pink liquid into another, larger jar. Outside, I saw a dust-covered car pull to a stop and a number of solemn-looking men get out. They went to the operating room first but did not stay there long. Soon they entered our ward.

"The idiots have finally arrived," Nikolai whispered jeeringly.

I watched the entry of the bunch—a general, a sergeant, a doctor carrying a medical bag, and a man in a black suit, whom Boris identified as a *politico,* a Soviet commissar. I was scared, but not as much as before; the reality was not as frightening as the fantasy. Finally, it was going to be over with—one way or another.

First, the orderlies—eleven of them—were made to line up for inspection. The doctor declared eight of them fit to rejoin their units. One of these was Yuri. Looking like prisoners being marched off to the gallows, the sergeant led them away.

"Now comes the little show," Mikhos whispered over his shoulder.

Severe and self-important looking, the group made its way up and down the aisles between the beds, with Swaroff, Rostovick, and the nurses on their heels. I could hear them firing off questions about one thing after another. Dr. Swaroff and the nurses seemed rather composed, but Dr. Rostovick was so nervous it was ridiculous. His movements were jerky and unnatural, and his high-pitched, annoying voice could be heard all over the room as he stammered out answers to questions.

The *politico* carried a briefcase and had a list of some kind. Now and then he would whisper something in the general's ear; the contingent would stop, the dark-suited man would open his case, and the general would pin a medal on the gown of a patient. Many of those receiving a medal seemed very pleased, but not a few appeared quite indifferent, almost scornful.

My hands started to sweat. The group wound its way down our aisle. In one of the first beds was a recent arrival, a boy who had suffered a head wound. On the top of his shaved head there was a circle of stitches, which for some reason had been left unbandaged, and he just lay there, totally limp and completely unaware of anything. Regardless, the general pinned a medal on this brain-dead boy—as though he still had a brain after all.

Nikolai and I exchanged glances but said nothing.

When I looked up again, the general was criticizing Dr. Swaroff about something. A heated discussion ensued, and the two walked away, out of earshot. My attention shifted to the dark-suited man, a stoop-shouldered, eerie-looking character. Taking advantage of the moment, he was flirting with Tamara, the pretty young girl with long, dark hair. She looked annoyed and was backing away, moving in my direction.

"How would you like to work *for me* at the commissariat?" he was asking her.

"Thank you, but I am needed here," Tamara replied.

"You would be doing very important work." He flashed a gold-toothed grin.

"I am *already* doing very important work, comrade. Don't you agree?" she said evenly, her dark, fathomless eyes fixed on him.

The man persisted. His intentions toward the girl were obvious; and he continued to pursue her openly despite the fact that he wore a wedding band, was old enough to be her father, and was making no progress at all with her.

His flirting was finally brought to an end by the return of Dr. Swaroff and the general. The two seemed to have patched up their differences and were now chatting amiably. After a handshake, the general again commenced decorating the wounded soldiers. A boy with a great mop of shaggy, blond hair was extremely excited to receive a medal. Startling me, the green-uniformed officer turned my way, but the *politico* tapped him on the shoulder and indicated the paralyzed man in the bed across the aisle.

"You have served the people of the Union of Soviet Socialist Republics well, comrade," said the general as he pinned on the medal. "Your nation is proud of you." He saluted.

The paralyzed man stared at the ceiling. "Take it off me, please," he said.

For a moment the general paused; then, as though he had not heard, he continued on.

"Take it off!" yelled the paralyzed man.

The general glanced sourly back at him. Then, after repeating his little speech, he decorated another soldier, conferred briefly with the *politico,* and then headed toward the exit.

"I don't want it, you stupid fool!" cried the man, his voice filling the ward. "Get it off me!"

The entourage stopped at the door. The general turned, showing a face red with anger and embarrassment, and looked back at the man. Time seemed to have stopped. The ward was silent. All eyes were on the general.

"Please," muttered the man.

The sound of footsteps broke the silence. Quietly, Tamara made her way to the paralyzed man and removed the medal. For an instant, the general looked as though he was going to charge at the girl and throttle her; but instead he suddenly turned and stormed from the room, the other men on his heels.

"Thank you," said the paralyzed man.

Tamara wiped his tears. She bent over, kissed him on the cheek, then made her way down the hall that led to the operating room, the medal in hand. For a long while after she had left, the ward remained silent.

Loss

Tamara Imanov. That was her full name. Everyone was sure there would be repercussions, that the girl would be punished in some way for standing up to the general. But the days passed and nothing happened.

Tamara was quite pretty. But her attractiveness was not entirely a consequence of her features; after what had happened at the inspection, I saw a very loving, strong, and good human being. Nothing is more alluring than a girl like that.

I had a crush on her—as did many others in the ward.

One day she came and took my temperature and pulse.

"Your temperature is fine," she said, "but your pulse is racing."

"I know," I said. I looked at where her hand was touching my wrist.

She blushed with understanding. "And why is your pulse racing?"

"Because of you," I said, afraid that I had been too bold. I smiled nervously.

Our eyes met. She gently patted my hand, then she was gone.

Early one morning I noticed Tamara peeking out the window not far from where my bed was situated. She did this over and over. It was nearing our lunchtime when suddenly her eyes lit up. Across the way were the stable and the abandoned dry-goods shop; and coming down the alley between the buildings was a young soldier—handsome, dark-haired, and unusually tall. He stood waiting in the alley when, from a side door of the hospital, Tamara suddenly emerged. She hurried across the road to the alley, where she and the soldier embraced. He gave her a blue scarf. They kissed, then, holding hands, walked down the street and disappeared from sight.

"Her boyfriend," said a boy across the way.

"Marusia's prettier," said another patient. He made a face. "But she's got a boyfriend, too—probably a dozen of them!"

I looked to where Tamara and her boyfriend had kissed. A sinking feeling inside, I frowned and looked away.

At this point, I had been in the hospital more than two weeks. Except for my abdominal wound, I felt pretty well. Though the tube was still in my side, very little of the pink gunk was coming out of me. I could sit up and even eat some solid food. My knee and head hardly bothered me at all.

Since coming to Alreni, supply trucks and other vehicles brought more wounded to the schoolhouse hospital on a fairly regular basis. They suddenly stopped coming. The reason, we learned, was that the Germans had retaken a large area of western Russia, and this had cut off all transport into Alreni. Now the hospital was running out of almost everything, and the patients began to suffer. At the same time, because there were fewer cases, we began to see more of our doctors and skilled nurses. Freed from doing almost nonstop surgery, they finally had more time to visit the wards.

I was awakened one afternoon to find Dr. Swaroff and a pudgy, moon-faced surgical nurse hovering near me.

"How are you feeling, boy?" asked Swaroff.

Due to the shortages, the dressing around my belly hadn't been changed in some time. The thing was sticky and crusty, and I'd been feeling nauseous off and on all day. I was about to tell him how miserable I felt, but then Tamara came over, and to Swaroff's question, I simply answered that I was fine. I wasn't about to whine like a little boy in front of her.

On Swaroff's instructions, she removed the bandage from my head. Then the chubby surgical nurse plucked the stitches from my scalp. Swaroff apologized. He and Rostovick had been so busy in the operating room that the sutures had been left in too long, he explained, and the wound had healed over to an extent that they were difficult to remove. It took quite a tug to get some of them out, and it felt like my scalp was being pulled apart. I clenched my jaw and tried not to let myself so much as flinch.

"I hope I'm not hurting you," said the stout nurse.

"*Nyet*," I said. My eyes were on Tamara—and the blue scarf around her neck, the one from her boyfriend.

Swaroff threw back the thin sheet, cut away the crusty bandaging around my abdomen, and began examining me. "The wound is healing nicely," he declared. "But this," he told the nurse, as he held up the red rubber tube, "should have been removed days ago!" Two strong, practiced fingers passed down on either side of the tube. "We're out of local anesthetics," he told me, "and I'm afraid this will hurt." He began to pull.

I closed my eyes against the pain. It felt as though a snake was wiggling around inside my gut. Suddenly it slithered wetly from the hole. I opened my eyes, and panting, lay back as Swaroff stitched the opening closed—without anesthetic. Sweat broke out on my forehead. Tamara patted it away with a cool cloth. "You are very brave," she said in her soothing voice.

I pursed my lips into something near a smile.

An orderly cut off the cast on my leg.

"It looks good," he said as he examined my knee. After touching it all over and asking where it was tender, he slowly bent the knee, testing the flexibility. At first, it felt as though my knee was going snap in half, but as Swaroff continued, the pain ebbed.

"Bed rest today," he told Tamara. "Then I want him walking with support."

"Yes, doctor."

Tamara and the other nurse rolled me onto my stomach so that Swaroff could work on the bullet's exit wound in my back. I let out a cry—not of pain, but of indignation. My rear end was exposed. Tamara must have seen hundreds of soldiers' backsides before. But it didn't matter—not to me. Furious and embarrassed, I quickly covered myself.

The pudgy nurse laughed. Tamara apologized. Me, I lay there on my stomach, mortified, as Swaroff removed the stitches from my back.

"You'll be up and about in no time," he told me, then left Tamara and the moon-faced nurse to rebandage me.

Lying facedown, I couldn't see the two as they worked, but I could tell the difference very clearly between Tamara's gentle touch and that of the other woman, whose fingers were like fat, stumpy sausages. Finally, I was rolled onto my back again, and the two left. I hurt, but I was glad to finally have the cast and tube gone. My mind was drifting when a drone of voices caught my attention. I turned to find Dr. Rostovick, a thermometer in hand and Katerina at his side, talking to my friend Nikolai.

"You have a fever," said Rostovick in his nervous, annoying voice.

Nikolai shrugged.

"Do you suffer from headaches?"

"Sometimes."

"And night sweats," continued Rostovick. "Do you sweat a lot, particularly at night?"

Nikolai nodded yes, at the same time shrugging it off again as being of no importance.

Rostovick, a worried expression on his twitchy face, looked at Nikolai's chart. "Four days without antibiotics," he muttered to Katerina. He gave her a knowing look, then pulled back Nikolai's sheets. Peering closely at the pants-like cast, he began pressing down on the plaster, which had a spongy, sort of soggy look about it.

"Does it hurt there?" Rostovick asked as he pushed down fairly hard on one spot.

"Yes, a little bit, Doctor," replied Nikolai.

"And there?" Rostovick's hands had moved to another area.

"No, Doctor."

"And how about there?"

"No, not at all."

Rostovick turned to Katerina, said something to her, and she hurried off, returning a few minutes later with two orderlies. On the doctor's instructions, they began cutting away at the huge cast. Almost immediately a putrid stench arose, and I didn't need to be a doctor to see that both of Nikolai's legs were badly infected. From midthigh down, they were swollen and streaked with black.

"Gaseous gangrene," said the doctor.

Nikolai pushed himself to a sitting position and stared down at his legs in horror and disbelief. "But they hardly hurt at all!"

"That's sometimes the case." Rostovick took a safety pin from his lapel then jabbed Nikolai's legs—gently at first, then harder.

Nikolai just watched. "I don't feel it!"

"The nerves, undoubtedly, are all but dead," Rostovick said, as he continued jabbing Nikolai's legs and feet with the pin. He looked at Katerina. "This is what happens as a result of not having a full regimen of antibiotics."

"What is wrong with my legs?" demanded Nikolai.

"They are badly infected, comrade."

All the color drained from Nikolai's face. "But I was sure they were getting better!" He lay back heavily.

Mikhos looked around from his bed at Nikolai, his forehead wrinkled up into a tight frown.

"We'll have to take them off," said Rostovick. "In order to save your life. And even then we may not be able to stop the—"

"Both my legs?" Nikolai stared wide-eyed at the ceiling.

"Yes, I'm afraid so."

"No, Doctor!" cried Nikolai. "What will I do without

my legs? I have a wife and children. I must take care of my family! I must work!"

"I'm sorry, comrade," said the doctor.

The operation was done that night. When Nikolai was returned to his bed, there were only stumps beneath the blanket.

In the morning I awoke to hear him crying softly to himself. He would not speak to me, Mikhos, or Boris—not to anyone.

That afternoon, Tamara and an orderly helped me from my bed. Between the two, with my arms around their shoulders, I walked almost the entire length of the ward. I was light-headed. My belly cramped up on me a bit. My knee felt weak but really hurt very little. All in all, I felt quite good; and walking with one arm around Tamara provided the pleasant illusion that she was my girl. But in another way, I felt horrid. As I walked, Nikolai's eyes were on me. I knew what he must be thinking, and I felt sick with guilt.

When I returned to bed, I averted my gaze from my legless friend. I just lay there, staring up at the ceiling—an ugly parade of thoughts going around in my head. The sun went down; the room began to darken. Around the ward, kerosene lamps were lit, turning the place to a soft mix of yellows, grays, and blacks. Surprising me, I felt a hand—Nikolai's—touch mine.

"It's all right, son," he said in a faint voice. "I'll make it."

I blinked at tears in my eyes. We did not look at each other. We simply lay there in the dark. He clasped my hand tightly and said good night.

A Letter from Home

If Nikolai could be strong, I decided, then so could I. I walked and exercised, often with Mikhos and Boris, who by then were also back on their feet. We grew stronger. Soon we were doing light chores, mostly around the kitchen. The work—cooking, serving, and washing tin plates—was not hard. And it reminded me of being home, of working in our restaurant, *Küche Apfelsine*, the Orange Kitchen. (My grandfather had originally painted the kitchen orange; grandmother made him paint over the orange, which she said was hideous; then they decided it made an interesting name for a restaurant.)

I often saved a bit of extra food for Nikolai. The color returned to his face, and little by little he seemed to be getting his strength back. Despite what he had been through—and what he had lost—he was still determined to get better.

One afternoon, while I was cutting up some carrots for a stew, feeling rather content, I idly commented that the kitchen reminded me of home.

Almost immediately, Mikhos was on me: "Ah! You are starting to remember!" he said excitedly. "Tell me, what else do you remember?"

I was dumbstruck and had no idea what to say. For an instant I was sure I had given myself away; then I collected my thoughts. I acted—playacted. "We owned a restaurant!" I told Mikhos exuberantly. "And I was always helping out!" I grimaced, as though deep in thought. I frowned falsely. "But that's all I remember."

Then and there I decided that it would be wise to show at least a little progress in coming out of my "amnesia." It would seem less suspicious. I told people that the name Aleksandr didn't mean anything to me, but I remembered more about the battle at Tarnapol. And I chose to remember that I was from Odessa, Russia, because I knew something of the area from stories my grandparents had told me. Perhaps more important, there was a minority of Silesians and Czechs in the region, and these people spoke with something similar to a German accent, sometimes even sprinkling their speech with German expressions. If I were to make any errors in the future, knowing these facts could save my life.

Supplies began arriving again, and so did new cases from the front. The beds began to fill up. When mine was needed, I was given a cot in a storage room with four other men. The place was hot and stuffy. After two miserable nights in there, the group of us was granted permission to move into a vacant house not far from the school-hospital. We were told it had once belonged to an eccentric, rather wealthy woman, the daughter of some famous czarist general. I had a room to myself—a parlor. In it stood an ancient piano without strings and a large gut-sprung sofa. The place was old, musty-smelling, and quite dreary, but it was a lot better than the storage room.

At five every morning an alarm clock in a room around the corner from mine rattled us awake. There was no need to get dressed; we slept in our clothes. Before sunrise the bunch of us would make our way the short distance through the streets of Alreni to the hospital. Sergo, our brain-damaged guard, was always on "patrol," usually out front, sometimes lurking near one of the abandoned buildings. Though he knew who we were, he always demanded that we identify ourselves. After we did so, he would salute and we would head inside, where we washed up, ate breakfast, and then went to work.

Mikhos and Boris were content working in the kitchen full-time. But more and more, I started working in the wards. I mixed plaster for casts; I emptied bed pans; I cleaned up messes; I took out dirty, blood-encrusted bandages and burned them in oil drums in a field near the hospital. The work was grueling—and hard on my bad knee—but at least I was doing something worthwhile. I was helping people instead of shooting them. The work had important bonuses, too. Out in the wards, I could check on Nikolai as often as I wanted, and I was around Tamara a lot of the time.

"X, please bring me blankets. Please heat up water to bathe the new boy. And when you're done, X, please try to get some nourishment—soup, porridge . . . anything—into the man who refuses to eat."

To this day, I can still hear Tamara's voice as she asked me—always sweetly and politely—to help out in some way or the other. I quietly did whatever she asked. Naturally, I had to help the other nurses and orderlies, too. But whenever possible, I was at Tamara's side, following her around the wards like her little puppy dog.

In late April, my identity papers, which I had to carry at all times, were amended and signed by Dr. Rostovick. Instead of a private, I was now *Aleksandr Dukhanov, medical orderly—temporary, 5th Service Regiment, Southwest Sector.*

Many of the patients were illiterate, and one of my jobs was to write letters for them while they dictated what they wanted me to say. I can still see the large pad of cheap paper on which I wrote with a stubby, square-shaped pencil. The letters were usually very simple and about the most ordinary sorts of things. The only difficult part about writing them was the need for the soldiers to inform their loved ones that they had been wounded, and trying to be cheerful and reassuring about it. But how does a young man tell his girl he can no longer father children, an aunt and uncle that he is so crippled he can no longer help out on the farm, or parents he is so disfigured they will probably not recognize him?

Letters—and sometimes parcels—arrived now and then for the patients and staff. Zoya and Rubin were in charge of distributing these. One afternoon in June, to my surprise, Rubin handed me a letter.

"A le-letter . . . for *me?*" I stammered. "But from whom? And how would anybody even know I am here?"

"As best we can," said Rubin, "Zoya and I locate the relatives of all the patients—especially those who have passed away or those, like you, who are unable to do so themselves."

"Thank you," I muttered as I took the letter.

"Hopefully it will help you remember more about yourself," Rubin added with a smile.

I sat down and finally mustered the courage to open the letter. It read:

> *My Dearest Son,*
>
> *My heart is filled with joy! Your sisters and I have not heard from you in so long and we feared the worst. But today we learned that you are alive, my darling son! We were upset to learn that you have been wounded but happy to hear that the doctors say you are recovering well. They say that you have memory loss but I will cook all your favorite dishes and that will surely bring back all of your memories! Anya*

and Ida and Grandpa are already planning a
big party and celebration for when you come
home. We cannot wait to hug you and smother
you with kisses and spoil you! Write to us!

> Love,
> Mama

Reading the letter made me terribly homesick. It felt
like it was a letter from my own mother. The letter also
overwhelmed me with guilt. No, I hadn't killed the
woman's son, but by taking his uniform and papers I had
filled his family with false hope and joyful anticipation of
a homecoming that would never be.

"What's wrong, X?" Tamara asked me late one evening.
I had just finished my shift and was sitting alone in the
kitchen, picking at my supper.

I just shrugged.

"You've always been so quiet . . . and different," she
said. "But not like this. Did something happen?"

I shook my head.

"Rubin said you received a letter today. Is that what's
bothering you?" She pursed her lips. "I hope I am not pry-
ing."

I showed her the letter.

"Why does it bother you, X?" she asked, after reading it.

"Because I don't know who these people are!" I
blurted, in a twisted-up way telling the truth. I don't even

124

really know who *I* am! I'm nobody!" Leaving my supper unfinished, I stormed from the kitchen out a side door.

"X!"

I stopped in the middle of the road. I turned.

Framed in a rectangle of light coming from the open door was Tamara. She slowly walked to me, then put her hand on my arm. "You're not nobody—not to me, you aren't," she said. Her expression was solemn, caring. "*Nyet.* No. Not to me," she said again, then hurried back inside.

What had Tamara meant by this? That night, I kept hearing Tamara's words over and over: "You're not nobody—not to me, you aren't." Long into the night, I lay there on the lumpy divan. Was it possible, I wondered, that Tamara cared for me? It seemed she did. But what *kind* of feelings were they? Was it pity she felt? Or friendship? Or, possibly, was it something more? Of course, she had a boyfriend in the army, I knew. But was Tamara also starting to have feelings of that kind for me?

I fell asleep with this wonderful fantasy in my head.

Sounds of the Past

June arrived. The days were warmer and longer.

Sometimes, in the early evening, I would go and sit in a grassy yard behind the school-hospital. It had once been a play area. Swings hung motionless, unused. A sandbox sprouted weeds. Big, wooden barrels had long ago been joined together to make a network of tunnels for kids to crawl through. Often I found myself wondering what the yard had been like before the war, with children laughing, yelling, and running around.

It was not a great deal unlike the play area in the primary school I had attended as a little boy back in Vilsburg.

Tamara joined me there one afternoon. At first our conversation was about the patients and ordinary matters we dealt with everyday. But then she asked me about myself—and if I remembered anything more. I told her as much as I could—about my family and other things I could safely share with her without giving myself away. Then I asked her about herself.

"I went to this school," she said.

"You did?" I said, surprised.

"Yes, when it *was* a school and not the place the war turned it into."

I followed her as she made her way across the yard. "My father built this," she said, putting a hand on one of the interconnecting barrels of the labyrinth. "He made it for the school. Dungeon World—that's what we called it. It was just about everybody's favorite thing. Lina, Marusia, Vlad, Katerina—all of us—we'd crawl around in there for hours!" She smiled at the memory. The smile sagged as she ran slender fingers over the warped wood of one of the barrels.

"Have you lived in Alreni all of your life?" I asked.

"Most of it. My parents moved here from Moscow when I was a baby." She grimaced. "Papa was in prison when I was born."

"In prison? For what?"

"For being an anti-Communist—an 'enemy of the state.'" A hard smile turned into a sneer. "He thought the Communists were idiots, and told them so. He had the guts to stand up to them."

"Like you did during the inspection—when you helped the paralyzed man?"

Tamara shrugged delicate shoulders.

"That was very brave," I said.

"Thank you." She sat down on a school bench, suddenly looking very young and vulnerable.

"How old are you?" I asked.

"Fifteen." She looked around the schoolyard. "Do you ever wish you were just a little kid again?"

"Yes, or at least have things back the way they were."

"Until I was twelve years old, or so, everything was so great."

"What happened when you were twelve?"

"That's how old I was when the lousy Germans invaded us. And right before that, Papa got in trouble with the Communists again. He wrote a pamphlet about Stalin betraying any of the good in communism. He wrote under a false name, but they caught him anyway. He was imprisoned again, this time for life—at the Peter and Paul Fortress in Leningrad."

I waited for her to go on.

"And while he was in prison, mother started seeing another man. We fought. More and more, I stayed with Katerina, at Zoya's house. One day, when I went home, mother wasn't there. She'd run off with the other man." Tamara scowled. "I don't know where she is—or really care."

"And you've been staying with Zoya ever since?"

She nodded.

I sat down on the bench, feeling too big and awkward for the thing. "Your father's still in prison?"

Anger flaring in her eyes, Tamara put a hand to her long hair and flipped it to one side. "No, he's dead."

I hung my head and then looked up frowning, waiting for her to continue.

"He was killed at Leningrad in 1941."

Sounds of the Past

"I'm sorry."

"It's not your fault. You didn't do anything."

I averted my gaze from hers.

"He was taken straight from prison and put in a death squad."

"What's that?" I asked, with genuine ignorance.

"The worst kept secret in Russia," replied Tamara. "Death squads were sent in ahead of the regular troops—armed with only grenades. They ran straight at the stinking, bloody Germans. They stepped on mines. They made the Germans use up ammunition. Those who get close enough threw their grenades. If they turned and ran, they were shot by their own troops." Her eyes hardened with rage. "And that's what they did to my father!"

"I'm so sorry, Tamara." I put a hand on her shoulder.

"I hate the Communists—just as much as I hate the Nazis," she said, her voice a lingering whisper.

"I do, too," I said.

In the old house where I lived there was an antique radio and record player. The thing, which ran on a gasoline-powered generator, was huge—about the size of a refrigerator, and about as heavy. None of us at the house could get it to work, but Rubin, after tinkering with it for a few hours one day, had both the radio and record player going. That afternoon, we hauled the contraption and a box of records to the hospital in an ambulance.

Not long after we had it set up in one of the wards, and Vlad and Oleg had mounted speakers in all the wards. Nothing was coming through on the radio. But then we tried out a record. It was incredible! No one had heard music in so long. And all of a sudden the whole hospital was filled with it.

It was classical music, Tchaikovsky.

Time had stopped. For a moment there was peace. For a moment there was beauty. Everyone was mesmerized. There were smiles on the faces of most of the patients and staff; and there were tears, too. Sergo came in from outside. With his scarred, dented-in head, he stood in place, swaying from side to side, holding his rifle as though it was his dancing partner.

It was the happiest I had ever seen the people in the hospital.

From then on, everyday from one-thirty to three-fifty P.M. there was a "symphony." At four o'clock there was usually a broadcast from Radio Moscow. The broadcasts, though biased and filled with propaganda, gave me some idea as to how the war was going. On June 6 the Allies had landed in France, at the beaches of Normandy. And while the British, Canadians, and Americans were coming from the west, the Russians were attacking from the east. Towns and cities all over Germany were being bombed to pieces, and I was sick with worry about my family.

When I try, I can still hear the broadcaster's voice—an irritating growl of bombast and political garbage. "Yesterday the glorious forces of the Soviet Union struck yet another mighty blow into the heart of the Fascist murderers, driving relentlessly westward as our fearless soldiers . . ."

One afternoon during one of those broadcasts the mail arrived. I was giving a sponge bath to a man whose arms looked as though only stitches were holding them together. I continued to work as many of the staff hurried over to see what had come, for themselves and the patients. As I was finishing up with the sponge bath, I saw Tamara emerge from the group around the mail bag with a letter in hand. Reading it, she made her way across the ward, the place filled with the sound of the broadcaster's voice. She suddenly stopped. A look of horror on her face, she hurried out a door.

I made my way outside. I found her across the roadway, sitting on the porch of the abandoned house with the cockeyed green door. Her head was back and her cheeks were wet with tears.

"Tamara?" I approached her tentatively.

She looked at me, then slowly removed the scarf from around her neck and wiped her eyes with it.

"Tamara?"

The letter fluttered to the ground. She spread the blue scarf wide in her hands and seemed to be studying it. "This is all I have left of him," she said. "Only five weeks ago—

in this very street—Isaak gave it to me before he left for the front."

I looked out at the empty street, in my mind seeing her sweetheart, the tall, handsome young man—then seeing them embrace. I'd been so jealous then. But now I found myself wishing him back, if only to take away Tamara's pain.

"Five short weeks, and now he's gone—dead." A sharp cry suddenly escaped her. She turned away, sobbing.

I just stood there, not knowing what to say or do. I waited until her crying finally stopped. She looked up; she reached out to me, and I helped her to her feet.

"I'm so sorry about your friend," I managed to say.

She cocked her head to one side. "'Friend'?"

"Boyfriend," I corrected myself.

"No, Isaak wasn't my boyfriend," she said.

"Oh," I muttered, far more surprised and confused than I think I sounded. "Then who was he?"

Her arms went around me. Weeping, she pressed her head against my chest. "He was my brother!"

"I'm so sorry," I said over and over, feeling a thousand different things at the same time, holding her and gently stroking her hair. "I'm so sorry, Tamara."

From the hospital came the broadcaster's voice: "And today, from the front, yet another victory for Mother Russia!"

Exclamation

For a long time after the day she received news of her brother's death, Tamara became very quiet. And different in other ways, as well. She went about her routine uncaringly, almost lazily, a blank expression on her face. At the same time, she did something that made me feel very good: She always seemed to want my company—so much so that I had the feeling she was following me everywhere I went, instead of me following her, as before. In the ward, the dining hall, the kitchen—she always seemed to be at my side. Still, she rarely spoke; and I did not know what this bond between us really meant. Did Tamara love me? I didn't know. I hoped so, but I was afraid that it wasn't really the kind of love that I wanted from her. A brother. I felt I had somehow become a substitute for her brother Isaak.

After learning about Tamara's loss, everyone else on the staff tried to help and comfort her. Her closest girlfriends were Katerina and Lina. Especially during the first days after Tamara got the letter, either Katerina or Lina would hug

Tamara as she cried. And every now and then they would go out of their way to say something comforting.

The two young women helped Tamara greatly. But I think it was Zoya, the grouchy, ugly head nurse, who helped her the most.

It happened in an odd way.

One afternoon Tamara accidentally dropped a liter of blood while taking it out of an ice chest in the operating room. I was on my hands and knees on the floor cleaning up blood and broken glass when Zoya charged over angrily and took Tamara aside.

At first Zoya lambasted Tamara for her clumsiness. We were in short supply of blood. Losing a whole liter of it was not an insignificant matter.

"You could cost someone their life!" Zoya exclaimed.

Tamara apologized, then started crying.

"There is no excuse for this kind of behavior!"

Tamara hung her head abjectly.

I expected Zoya to keep on with the tirade and show no pity. That was usually her way. Instead, to my surprise, she suddenly took a new tack, turning things around so that the incident could be used to help Tamara.

"We have all suffered great losses in this war," Zoya said, her tone suddenly softer and kinder.

"I know," Tamara replied. "But now my whole family is gone!"

"You have suffered a great deal—as we all have. We all have reasons to go around feeling sorry for ourselves.

Exclamation

But we can't," said Zoya. "We have to keep going. We have patients, and they need our help."

"Yes, I understand, but—"

"No! You don't understand!" Zoya exclaimed. "You've lost your father and now your brother. The two of you were very close, and his death has hit you hard. But it is time to get over it. And the only way to get over it is to stop thinking about yourself, Tamara. Start thinking about the patients."

Tamara, head hanging, nodded.

Zoya lifted her chin. Smiling, she continued. "I am telling you this not just for the sake of the patients, Tamara dear. I am telling it for your sake. Not until you get back to caring for patients with all your heart and soul will your own pain begin to go away." Zoya let go of her chin, but continued smiling. "Do you understand what I'm telling you?"

"Yes," Tamara replied softly.

Zoya patted Tamara's arm. "Good, then you will be okay."

Little by little, Tamara emerged from her despair. She threw herself into her work with more energy and compassion than ever. She was not exactly the same person as before. She was something better.

In the mornings, I began getting up extra early. And instead of walking to the hospital with my friends, I would make my way through town to the house where Tamara lived with Zoya and Katerina, and walk to the hospital with her.

One morning we arrived earlier than usual. We stoked and refilled the ancient wood-burning stove, and after tea and a little fruit, we went to work—Tamara in the wards, me in the operating room. The hideous stainless-steel surgical table—I had begun scrubbing it down when Zoya and Katerina arrived. Yawning, I called out a sleepy hello.

"Get everything in top shape." Zoya had come into the operating room. "There is going to be an inspection today."

Fear swept over me. "Oh," I said, the word a hard knot in my throat. "At what time?"

"They are supposed to come around noon. But who knows when the idiots will show up." Zoya gave me a pat on the back. "I hope they don't take you."

Then she was gone, leaving me frozen, a horrifying panoply of thoughts going around in my head. I wanted to scream. I wanted to run. I didn't know what to do. I continued scrubbing—in my mind seeing myself standing for inspection, then being led off. *I won't go—not this time!* I decided. *I'm not fighting in their stinking army, or ours.*

I lugged a bucket of filthy, red-tinged water outside and poured it onto the ground. I rinsed it and refilled it from the iron spigot, working the pump handle angrily, then made my way into the kitchen. I set the pail on the wood-burning stove, waiting for the water to heat. Tamara came in. She put a hand on my shoulder, then, surprising me, she reached up and kissed my cheek. For a moment, our mouths lingered close.

"Try not to worry, X," she said. "You've been here less than three months. You're not fully healed."

I tried to force a smile.

"Try not to worry," she said again, then began mixing porridge in a bowl.

I was lost in thought when I realized the water had begun to boil. I hefted the heavy pail off the burner. It caught on something and tipped. Scalding water hit my arm. *"Ach sheisse!"* I screamed in pain—in German. *"Mein Gott!"*

Tamara's head jerked up, her eyes suddenly wide. "Oh, my God!" She came toward me—then backed away. "My God, who are you? What are you?"

Later, Katerina smeared salve on my scalded left arm, and wrapped it in heavy bandaging. Tamara watched, her expression dark, unreadable, her eyes fixed on mine. Feeling transparent, all my secrets revealed, I stared back.

"Is something wrong?" said Katerina, looking from Tamara to me. "What's wrong?"

The inspection took place late that afternoon. I stood rigid with nerves, my burned arm throbbing, as the team of inspectors examined the orderlies—Boris and Mikhos, and I, and seven others.

Out of the corner of my eye, I saw Tamara whisper something to Zoya, who shook her head and opened her hands in a gesture of futility. I turned my head. I looked out at the ward, and at my friend Nikolai, sitting legless in a wheelchair. He crossed himself.

"What are his wounds?" a green-uniformed officer demanded as he stood before me.

Rostovick explained.

An unsmiling woman—perhaps a doctor from headquarters—examined me, and then Boris, the last in line. The inspectors conferred. The woman returned. Her gaze traveled down the line of us, and for a moment came to rest on my bandages. "All except these two," she said tonelessly. She pointed at Mikhos and me.

I hung my head, sick with shame, as Boris, Konstantine, and the others were herded away.

Flight

A white-painted bus.

On it, severely crippled—but "recovered"—men were taken away late one afternoon. Home—that was their destination. Nikolai and I smiled through our tears as we said good-bye.

The bus groaned away, pitching from side to side.

The other orderlies and nurses who had helped them board the thing watched as it turned a corner, and then was gone. The others went inside; Tamara lingered for a moment, then followed them. I sat down on one of several wooden crates the bus had brought. It was a warm afternoon, but my heart felt frozen. I looked out at Alreni, at a desolate sprawl of wooden buildings extending several kilometers over thinly forested flatland. Beyond lay dark, brooding mountains, their peaks lit lavender by a failing sun.

———

In mid-August, a broadcast from Radio Moscow informed us that the Germans had launched a new offensive. We hardly needed to be told. In the distance we had already begun hearing the rumble of artillery fire.

We knew what to expect next.

Before the week was out, ambulances, carts, and military vehicles of every sort began arriving with wounded men. More than half of the new arrivals were from southern, Asiatic regions of the Soviet Union, making it extremely difficult to communicate with them. There were so many of them, and we were so desperate for transportation, that even old cars were pressed into service; and these would come puttering to us directly from the front with their bloodied passengers.

The hospital quickly filled to overflowing. Men with gaping lacerations, blasted limbs, and horrid burns—the wounded were everywhere. Dr. Swaroff and Dr. Rostovick, the nurses, and the rest of us were overwhelmed trying to care for all of these men. And still more kept coming.

For the first time, I began pulling a double shift. Instead of working just a nine-hour day, we all worked twelve hours—six on the day shift and six at night.

Between Tamara and I there was a wall of silence; we hardly spoke. I didn't know what she was thinking—or what she would do. At any time, she could turn me in. I wasn't sure if I cared.

Flight

———

The fighting came closer. As we worked, artillery rounds sometimes shook the building. We could even hear the snip and snap of rifle fire coming from the forested hills beyond Alreni.

Orders came down. The hospital, as well as the town, was to be evacuated, starting immediately. All our wounded were to be transported to Tredsk, a town some thirty kilometers to the east.

Fighting was already breaking out in Alreni as trucks, ambulances, cars, and old, battered buses arrived to take us away early one afternoon. Working at a frenzied pace, we loaded all of our most seriously injured patients on board. We had started loading the walking wounded and medical supplies and equipment, when the wooden buildings across the way erupted, showering us with flaming splinters. Somewhere nearby a machine gun hammered; grenades banged in quick succession.

"Go!" I screamed, slapping the side of a bus.

It was already moving.

"X!"

I saw Tamara in the back of a flatbed truck filled with patients, and then I was running after the thing. Sergo pulled me aboard. A blind man kept yelling: "What's happening?" Other patients cried in pain as the heavy truck bucked and jolted along the rutted road.

For a moment our convoy seemed to be leaving the fighting behind—as well as Alreni, much of which was now in flames. We were passing through a wooded area when we heard intermittent gunfire coming from off to our left. The back window of a car in front of us shattered and black smoke began pouring from beneath the vehicle. In a great eruption of flame and flying debris, it exploded. I saw several Russian soldiers running through gales of smoke and dust, gunshots chasing them. Some of the shots punched holes in the cab of the truck as it swerved around the burning debris of the car. More shots rang out; Katerina seemed to swoon, to collapse almost gently, ladylike onto her arm. Her eyes closed; blood pooled out from beneath her.

"Oh God, no!" shrieked Zoya.

I looked at Zoya kissing the translucent face of Katerina, crying, almost howling; then Tamara was holding both of them, the dead, beautiful girl and her aunt, Zoya, soaked with blood from her niece.

I think it was a mortar round that hit the bus behind us. The front two thirds simply disintegrated. The rear of it spun around, spilling several of its occupants—Dr. Rostovick and three or four patients.

Spewing gravel, our truck skidded to a stop.

I scrambled into the back of the bus. An orderly walked past me, his face freckled with tiny cuts from broken glass. No one else in the bus was alive.

For a moment, there was relative quiet.

Flight

What was left of the convoy was headed away without us.

Those who had been in the rear of the bus, and had survived, were sitting on the ground in a daze. Zoya, Tamara, Mikhos, and I helped them aboard our truck. A group of terrified townspeople, mostly women and children, emerged, and we helped them on as well. The truck was now packed with dazed and wounded people; there was no room for the rest of us. I slammed my palm against the door of the truck, surprised by my new role as leader. "Go!" I ordered.

Bullets kicked up powder puffs of dust in the road; one bullet hit a rear tire of the truck. Tilted to one side, the vehicle lumbered away.

"We have to get out of here!" Mikhos yelled.

Zoya, Mikhos, Tamara, and I scrambled into the woods. Two Germans ran past; they saw us but kept going. Sergo loomed into view. I grabbed Tamara's hand. All of us ran. Somewhere behind us, a machine gun was chattering. Mortar shells exploded in the woods, off to our left.

"Down!" I screamed.

We hugged whatever protection the land provided. The thunderclaps of mortar rounds pounded the woods, spraying us with dirt, rock, and chunks of wood. A tree snapped at the base; in flames, it fell. I heard Mikhos scream.

"Mikhos!" I cried, and for a moment saw him, trapped beneath the blazing, fallen pine, now a part of the flames. Zoya dragged me away, and then Tamara was beside me, too. We were running, Sergo ahead of us. Off to our left, spears of flame were shooting upward and outward from the forest. Instantly, it became a swirling wall of flame. We ran, waves of superheated air chasing us. There was a sudden crackling roar directly above us as towering firs burst into flames.

"There!" Sergo was pointing, screaming.

Off to our right, and down a steep, pine-needle-covered incline, was a broad ravine. We ran, fell, then skied down the slope, tumbling together into the ravine—a dry streambed.

The world lit with intense light, intense heat. I saw the red of the fire through closed lids. Flames roared overhead.

Then they were gone.

I opened my eyes to blackness, to smoke. And through tearing eyes I saw thousands of red-hot little curls of burnt pine needles drifting downward.

The fire continued burning, but it was far beyond us now—great tendrils of flame leapfrogging, looping away through the forest.

The three of us picked ourselves up. Our clothes were pocked with burn holes; our hair and brows were singed. We were coughing; the cut in my hand was bleeding; our eyes were red and burning.

But still we could see that something was wrong.

There were only three of us. Zoya was gone.

Part Three

Into the Void

We backtracked over scorched, blackened land, searching for Zoya. The hills looked like huge heaps of charcoal; the trees like fat, blackened poles. Now and then a previously untouched sprig, bush, or clump of grass would erupt in flame.

We found Zoya's body curled up in a ball near a rocky outcropping. With our hands, we dug a shallow grave, then covered it with stones. Tamara's eyes glistened with tears as she, Sergo, and I stood over Zoya's grave.

In the near distance we heard artillery. Nervous, on the lookout for danger, we headed in the opposite direction. No one spoke. The only sound was the shuffling of our feet as we plodded along through thick ash. We choked on thin, powdery clouds of the stuff constantly being kicked up as we walked. It got in our eyes, mouths, and noses. The whole earth, it seemed, stank of fire; and our bodies, too, were permeated with the stench. Overhead, a warm sun bore down. Black rivulets of sweat dribbled down our faces, necks, and arms. Tamara's hair was singed and heat-curled. The back of my right hand was brown-red with cooked blood from a cut. We had no food or water, no supplies of any kind, and no equipment other than Sergo's rifle and a small pocketknife he carried.

We came upon a deer that had been killed by the fire. It may sound revolting, but the animal was already cooked and ready to eat, which we did. Sergo then butchered it as best he could with his small knife. We set off again, each of us carrying a leg of venison.

We crossed a grassy plateau, wary of any troops that might be in the area. A steep, pine-covered slope gave way to a broad valley and then to marshy flatland. A putrid odor rose from the muck through which we found ourselves slogging, foul water welling up underfoot and seeping into our shoes and boots. Clouds of mosquitoes and almost invisible mites stung us relentlessly.

Thirst began to drive us crazy. All around us was water—stagnant, slimy, and covered with yellow-green skins of algae.

"No, Sergo."

Sergo had dropped to his knees and was about to drink the wretched stuff.

"No," said Tamara again. "That water is like poison." She grabbed him gently by the collar and pulled him to his feet.

After crossing an especially large and rank-smelling bog, we found ourselves stopped by a dense thicket of cane. We made a detour up a short, rocky incline, and were greeted by a soothing breeze whispering through a forest of tall, gray-barked oak trees. Shortly we came to a small stream. We drank thirstily and washed our hands and faces in the cool, clean water.

Feeling better, we got underway again. As I moved along, eyes fixed on my feet, I found myself studying small patches of sunlight on the ground. They changed shape, expanded and contracted each time the leaves stirred overhead. Sometimes a shaft of light would dart like a yellow arrow across the ground, then retract; golden specks would appear, grow in size, jump around, then suddenly vanish. I recalled a game I had played as a boy. On a hike through the woods, a friend of mine named Kurt Olsen and I had arranged a race in which we were not allowed to step on the spots of sunlight.

"What are you doing?"

I looked at Tamara and was suddenly embarrassed. Without realizing it, I had been stepping over spots of sunlight.

Unsmiling, Tamara arched a brow in question. "What was all that about?"

Blushing, I explained about the boyhood game. "I didn't even realize what I was doing," I said. "I forgot myself for a second."

"How does a person forget what they don't remember?" she mused, the comment tinged with sarcasm.

"It's a quickly acquired skill—under difficult circumstances," I replied.

The trees began to thin. Spindly saplings replaced the huge, old oaks and elms. We found ourselves picking our way down a hot, winding slope, grabbing hold of saplings and bushes for support. The sound of rushing water greeted our ears. Ahead, through the trees, we spotted a waterfall—several of them. A granite cliff had been worn away into what looked like four or five chimneys set close together. Water gushed over them and spilled down between them into a large, deep pond.

The three of us tossed our shoes and socks aside on the shore; then, in our filthy clothes, we waded right in until the wonderfully cool water was almost up to our necks. We bathed, letting the water wash away the grime and stink of smoke, and ease the itching from our mosquito bites.

Afterward, we sat and let the sun dry us.

"Where are we?" asked Tamara in a monotone. "Where are we headed?"

"Southwest," I told her. "That's all I know."

"Perhaps toward German lines?"

"I'd prefer not, since technically I'm a deserter." The tension between us was hard, palpable. I tried to soften it. "Perhaps somehow we can make it to Switzerland, or some neutral country."

"I want to go to America!" Sergo suddenly exclaimed.

Into the Void

Tamara and I exchanged glances, tacitly communicating our mutual reaction that the notion was absurd. She got to her feet. "Yes," she said, a sardonic edge to her voice. "Yes, let's go to America!"

"Oh, good!" exclaimed Sergo.

My Countrymen, My Enemy

For the next three days we traveled through forest followed by more forest. There were no towns or villages, nor any trace of civilization. We ate the last of our venison. We were tired and hungry. At night we shivered with the cold; during the day we were broiled by the sun.

Finally, late one afternoon, we found ourselves at the edge of a freshly plowed field. In the center a farmer worked slowly with a plow and a sway-backed horse. We eased back into the woods and discussed what to do, finally agreeing that Sergo and Tamara should wait for me while I went to talk to him.

The farmer did not see me until I was only a few meters from him. His head jerked in fear at my approach. At first he looked as though he was going to run away. But in the next instant he fumbled an old revolver from his waistband. "Who are you?" he demanded in oddly accented Russian.

"I'm a medical orderly," I told him. "I don't mean you any harm. I just need a little help."

"I can't help anybody." The old man looked like a reptile. His skin was tough and weathered into little folds and scaly crisscrosses of wrinkles. His eyes bulged and, like a lizard's, seemed to move independently of each other. "Go away. Leave me alone!"

"I'm lost," I said. "At least tell me where I am."

"Only if you leave here—and quickly! These are dangerous times!"

I nodded.

After learning as much as I could from the strange-looking old man, I returned to Sergo and Tamara.

"We are in the Ukraine," I told them. "About eight kilometers from the Czechoslovakian border. There has been heavy fighting in the area for months."

We headed off. Not wanting the farmer to see us, we circled the field through the woods, eventually emerging on a dirt road. We hurried along it, nervous, wary.

At first I didn't know what I was seeing. We were passing an orchard. High up in leafless trees, items of clothing fluttered, as if they had been washed and hung out to dry. Then we saw shell craters—blasted-out circles in the orchard—and bodies. Many were naked, and I realized the people had literally been blown out of their clothes. I spotted a Russian soldier, his broken body twisted against a tree. Nearby lay two more. Sergo joined me. We went through backpacks, finding food, clothing, bedrolls, and other items. We also found two rifles—only one of which was still usable—and more ammunition than we could carry.

Perhaps an hour later we found ourselves approaching the ruins of a town, the roadway paved with bits of shrapnel. We passed abandoned trenches and machine-gun nests; and everywhere there was wrecked, rusting equipment—cannons, tanks, and vehicles of various kinds. Among these was a colossal, fire-blackened German troop carrier with several rows of seats for soldiers. The sides of the thing were pierced with thousands of bullet holes, giving the contraption the appearance of some sort of huge, wheeled sieve.

The houses and other structures in the town had been turned into one long, mountainous woodpile—all of them reduced to broken planks and boards piled every which way amidst other rubble. Near the end of town was a small hotel, a two-story affair of battered brick and plaster. A winding stairway led nowhere, abruptly ending in midair. Resting on a ragged-edged platform, once part of the flooring of an upstairs room, was a bed. Nearby was a closet in which clothes hung neatly.

A kilometer or more from the town, we came to a shell-pocked stone structure bearing a brass sign reading Pedagogical College.

"It's getting late," said Tamara. "We're tired."

"Yes, tired," said Sergo, a smile revealing decayed and missing teeth.

An oversize door squeaked on its hinges. We filed in through a small lobby and then into the silent ruins of an auditorium. Most of the wooden seats had been torn up, probably for fuel. On a sagging stage, a huge scarlet curtain hung lopsided.

"This place was used by German soldiers," said Tamara.

"And just about everybody else," I added.

On the walls were comical drawings, mostly obscene but not badly drawn, and there were names and messages by the dozen—in German, Ukrainian, Czech, and Polish. Overall, the place gave the impression of a trash dump. Everywhere, there was litter—broken furniture, empty food tins, and wine bottles, and dank, rotting clothing. There were several large oil drums that had been used as makeshift heaters and stoves.

We opened the tins of food we had found in the Russians' packs, and ate hungrily. We pulled shirts, jackets, socks, and blankets from the packs. We put the clothing on; we covered ourselves with the thin blankets, and were soon fast asleep.

Early the next morning we were off again. Tinged orange by a rising sun, a cool fog blotted out the world. From somewhere far off we heard artillery fire, and from behind suddenly came the sound of heavy footsteps. We hurried off the road; moments later we watched as a long, stretched-out column of weary-looking German soldiers tramped past. In the eerie haze, they looked spectral, like a troop of ghosts.

My palms were wet with perspiration, my mouth dry. I was scared to death of them. I wore a Russian shirt, had a Russian pack on my back, and carried a Russian Simonova rifle. My own countrymen had become my enemy.

Their footsteps faded.

Then they were gone.

I breathed easier. We headed off, past the burnt ruins of a church, and then across fields of dead grass. Ahead, through the mist, I saw a dark-haired little girl sitting on the stoop of a farmhouse. In her lap was a kitten. Smiling, the little girl picked up one of the animal's tiny paws and waved it at us.

"Dobraye utro. Guten Morgen." Good morning, she said to us, first in Russian, then in German.

"Dobraye utro," said Tamara with a smile.

Around midmorning, the fog finally burned off; a spectacular day opened before us. All was quiet and serene, the sky an electric blue spotted with puffy, stationary-looking clouds. The artillery fire we had heard earlier had stopped. As we waded through knee-high grass down a long, winding slope, everything seemed almost too tranquil and beautiful to be true. Several large areas of the slope were covered with colorful sweeps of wild flowers in bloom. Reds, whites, pinks, and purples mingled, quietly ruffled by a soft breeze.

"It's so pretty, isn't it?" mused Tamara, wandering a bit ahead of Sergo and me.

I was about to agree; my eyes happened to fall on a sight that sickens me to this day. Amidst the flowers, sticking out from a grassy mound, were two skeletonized arms from which bits of rotten cloth were hanging. The arms looked as though they were reaching out from the ground for help.

"So beautiful," said Tamara, having walked right past them without noticing.

A pleasantly warm morning became an unbearably hot afternoon. The pack and heavy Simonova rifle began weighing on me. My bad knee ached; I began to lag. Tamara, the Russian army jacket tied around her waist, offered to carry the pack for a while.

I declined her offer.

"Don't be a fool." Stopping me, she quietly slipped the straps off and took the pack.

"Thank you," I said, and then helped her on with the thing.

For the rest of the day we traded the pack back and forth.

The afternoon waned. Finally, the heat began to abate as we found ourselves on a trail leading down through acres upon acres of dead, unharvested corn. Sergo, who had been ahead of us, stopped; he waited for us to catch up, and then fell in stride.

"When do we get to America?" There was a pouting tone to his voice. He turned his dented head toward me. "How much farther is it to America?" he asked.

"Quite a ways ahead," I said, not wanting to tell him it was thousands of kilometers away, and across the sea. "We have a lot of walking ahead of us. We have to keep pushing on. The faster we go, the sooner we'll get there."

"Oh, okay," he said like a child. "I'll make it. I'm a good walker." He strode ahead, as if to prove he was a good walker and was going to get to his magical destination as fast as possible.

We were making our way down the trail through a cornfield—the dead, head-high cornstalks creating sort of a walled-in walkway. Ahead, at the bottom of the slope, was an open area, and beyond that a dark, cool-looking forest.

"Wait up, X." Tamara had stopped. She pulled off the backpack and, sitting on it, was taking off a shoe.

I made my way back to her and waited as she shook a pebble out of her shoe.

"Are we getting closer?" called out Sergo from a dozen meters or so ahead of us. He had stepped up onto a rocky hummock in the middle of the trail. His rifle yoked across his shoulders, he was squinting, looking off into the distance as though trying to spot America.

A gunshot ruptured the quiet. Sergo staggered backward as his rifle went flying. He landed on his side; his rifle, its stock smashed by a bullet, lay several meters away. Dazed, he was looking at a bloodied hand and trying to get up when a German soldier rose into view in the cornfield. Crunching out from it, he moved slowly toward Sergo. Grinning, he was aiming his rifle at the helpless man.

Sergo's terrified eyes swiveled in our direction.

The German's gaze followed Sergo's. He saw us, but his rifle was still pointed down.

Mine was pointed at him. I fired.

A small, red stain appeared on the soldier's shirt. An expression of surprise on his face, he looked down, then brushed at the stain as though he had just spilled something on himself and was trying to get it off. He dropped his gun, raised his hands, said "don't shoot" in German, then crumpled in a heap.

"X!" Tamara was standing, pointing.

A second German pushed out from the tall corn. I fired. His helmet flew off. He fell and lay there stunned, half-conscious.

"Wo seid ihr zwei?"

Far off, an anxious voice was asking, "Where are you two?" in German.

I looked around, but saw nothing. I looked to where Sergo had been, and then saw his feet disappear as he crawled into the corn and vanished.

"Was ist passiert?"

A German had yelled, "What's happening?" I heard

159

several more voices, and then the sound of rustling, crackling movement. Through grass and spindly cornstalks, perhaps two hundred meters away, German soldiers were hurrying in our direction. The grass and corn there were shoulder-high, and I could see little of the soldiers except for their bobbing helmets. And if I could not see them very well, I realized, then they probably could not see us or what had happened in the high-walled pathway through the cornfield. Still, they had heard the gunshots and it would only be moments before they were on us. I had to do something—*think* of something—or we would be dead.

"Stay back!" I yelled to them in German. "*Anhalten!* It's a trap!"

Tamara was staring at me, terror and confusion in her eyes.

"*Deckung! Es ist ein Trick!*" I shouted. Get down! "*Alle zurückbleiben!*"

Helmets sank from view.

"Follow me!" I hissed at Tamara in Russian.

We raced past the two fallen Germans. And for a time the cornstalks of our walled-in pathway were high enough to hide us. We had almost made it to the forest when the pathway abruptly ended. We stopped. Between the forest and us was now a long stretch of open ground. Tamara looked toward the forest, then to me, with her eyes asking me what we should do.

"We'll have to run for it!" I panted. I glanced back at a grassy patch of hillside. I saw a helmet; then, like some sort of surrealistic garden, scores of German soldiers suddenly sprouted on the grassy slope.

"There!" yelled one of them. "*Da drüben!* Down there!"

A single gunshot popped.

"Run!" I yelled, and then we were racing across the stretch of open ground.

From behind us came the *brrrrp* of an automatic weapon. Bullets snapped past. There were shouts in German, the sound of fast, noisy footfalls coming down the hill, and then a flurry of rifle fire. Tamara and I stumbled into the forest as bullets punched into trees and kicked up little sprays of dirt and gravel. "Get them!" screamed a voice not far behind us.

Tamara and I were now racing through the forest. Bullets lashed at the vegetation overhead, showering us with shredded leaves. We zigzagged, then scrambled off in a different direction, along a dry streambed. There was another burst of automatic weapons fire, but it was behind us and far off to our right.

The Germans, it seemed, had lost our trail.

Gasping for breath, we slowed our pace. We left the streambed and found ourselves picking our way through tangles of briar and heavy brush. I realized I no longer had my rifle, and wondered vaguely where I'd left it. The pack, too, was gone—left back on the pathway through the cornfield.

The ground became muddy and soft. We hopped over a tiny, brackish pond, pushed our way through reedlike vegetation, then moved quickly along a narrow pathway— perhaps an animal trail.

We seemed to be alone.

But then the hair suddenly stood up on the back of my neck.

"Welchen weg?" "Which way?" an out-of-breath voice huffed.

Terrified, Tamara and I stood riveted in place. The voice was in front of us and only a few meters away.

"Ich weiss nicht." "I don't know," responded another soldier.

"Forget it," said the first voice.

Neither Tamara nor I moved. We stared. No more than ten meters away, two German soldiers stepped into view. If they had turned around, they would have seen us. Instead, they continued on, headed back the way they had come. Crunching away noisily through brush, they disappeared into the woods.

To this day, I do not know how the two got ahead of us. I do not know how they could have missed seeing us. But that is what happened.

For what seemed an eternity, Tamara and I continued to stand stock-still. Then it was as though we came out of a state of paralysis, and together we crawled into an umbrella-like enclosure of green shrubbery and stumpy, drooping willows. We knelt on moist, springy ground. We waited. We listened. Now and then we could hear voices and footsteps—headed away from us.

Finally, all was quiet. Still, we were afraid. We remained in our hiding place, not speaking, not moving.

The air became cooler. Shadows began to lengthen. Night fell. In silence, Tamara untied the jacket from around her waist and spread it on the ground. We curled up together against the cold. A bat—or perhaps some sort of night bird—flapped by overhead. My head pillowed on my hand, I looked at Tamara. Her eyes were on me; then they closed.

Strangers

Tamara was gone when I awoke. I was in a panic, a thousand thoughts going through my head—until I spotted her a short distance off. Below, in a narrow cleft between low ridges, was a stream—a series of small ponds, really, connected by a snaking, little waterway.

"Good morning," I said when I had made my way down to her.

"Good morning," she said quietly, her eyes on the pond beside which she sat.

"When I woke up and didn't find you," I said, "I was afraid you'd left. I thought you'd headed for home, or something."

"What home?" she said flatly. She looked up. "You were worried that I was gone? Why would that matter to you?"

"Because it would," I said, suddenly angry. "It would matter a lot."

She looked at me thoughtfully for a moment, then returned her gaze to the water.

I knelt by the pond. I cleaned up cuts and scrapes,

washed my hands and face, and drank my fill of water—
my breakfast. I flicked water off my hands, then I dried my
face and hands on the Russian tunic I was wearing.

"You were very smart, very brave, yesterday," said
Tamara.

I said nothing in response.

"Sergo got away safely because of you, and so did
we." Looking at the water, she moved a finger across the
surface as though drawing a design on it.

"I hope Sergo made it," I said.

"The first German, the one that shot Sergo, is dead,
isn't he?"

"I think so."

"What did you yell in German to them?" she asked
without looking up. "How would you know what to say?"

I wondered how much she really knew, how much she
had already figured out. Then I exhaled the truth. "I'm a
German. I was wounded and ended up behind Russian
lines. I am—I *was*—a German soldier."

She grimaced, then slowly nodded in understanding.

"After that morning, when I burned myself . . ." My
words trailed off.

"I knew then," she said, her voice hard. "But I didn't
know for sure *what* I knew—only that you were German."

"Why didn't you turn me in?"

I didn't know what to do." She was scrutinizing me. "I
still don't."

"Do what you have to."

"What's that?"

"Survive."

A cool morning wind whispered through the culvert, tossing and rustling the leaves of bank-side trees. Most of the trees were leaning inward, as if trying to hear what we were saying.

"You fooled me for a long time. You fooled everyone."

I looked at her but said nothing.

"Who are you?"

"I'm really not sure."

"What's that supposed to mean?"

"That I'm a little confused—about who I am, I mean." I smiled broadly, offensively so.

She slapped her hands against her knees, then got to her feet. "Your amnesia—that was a lie, wasn't it?"

"Yes."

"And your grandparents," she scoffed. "Your *Russian* grandparents. That was a lie, too!"

"No, that part *was* true," I said, fighting my own welling anger "They *are* Russian, and I happen to love them very much! They emigrated to Germany."

"You had started to remember, you said. You told me so many things. The restaurant. You lived above a restaurant."

"We did—we *do*. Our apartment is above our restaurant—the *Küche Apfelsine,* the Orange Kitchen." I shrugged. "But the restaurant is in Germany, in the town of Vilsburg."

Anger flaring in her eyes, she put a hand to her long hair and flipped it to one side. "Start over," she said demandingly. "Who are you?"

I looked down at my identity number, stenciled in blue ink on the top of my orderly's smock. "I am," I said, "Aleksandr Dukhanov, medical orderly—temporary, Fifth Service Regiment, Southwest Sector."

Tamara glowered. "Tell me!"

"Is that an order?"

Her tone softened. "*Please* tell me."

I started at the beginning. I told her everything. I told her my name. I told her about my family, about Vilsburg, about being in the *Jugend,* about being drafted as a so-called interpreter, and ending up on the front lines. I told her about killing Russians at the battle of Tarnapol, and about the Russians executing German soldiers. I described things I had seen, awful things.

She sat quietly.

I told her about the Jewish people, and about the deaths of Rosy Cheeks, Hals, Oskar, and of others whose names I never knew. There were tears in my eyes. Embarrassed, I brushed them away.

"A Nazi crying," she said, her tone noncommittal. "Something I never expected to see."

"Yes, I *am* crying," I said, biting my words, trying to control a sudden surge of fury. "I admit that I am capable of crying. But I am *not* a Nazi—a member of the *National*

167

Socialist party! Most Germans aren't, including my family and I!"

"Oh," said Tamara, a genuine look of surprise on her face.

"The Nazis control our bloody government and even bloodier military. They give the orders. We do what we are told—mostly because we are weak." I picked up a stone and flipped it into the stream.

"Yesterday you killed a German."

"I'm not proud of it."

"You killed him to protect me and Sergo, two Russians."

"And to protect me—a German." I held out my hands in two claws of futility. "I don't want to kill *anybody!*"

"I don't even know you, do I?"

"Then we are both confused on the same subject!"

"You were good. You were so good with the patients. You cared, or seemed to."

"I *did* care!"

She looked at me thoughtfully. "But they were Russians."

"So what?" I snapped.

Her dark eyes blinked.

"So they were Russians. Russians, Germans—what's the difference!"

She looked at me. The only sound was the soft, redundant music of the stream.

Skeletons in the Forest

We followed the stream, expecting it to feed into a river. Instead, it ended in a brackish, dead-looking pond. We backtracked; we took what we thought was a shortcut and found ourselves entering a deepening forest. Sun sparkled through the green canopy high overhead, like stars on huge Christmas trees.

"Where are we?" asked Tamara.

"Lost, I'm afraid."

A formation of planes droned somewhere far above. I looked up through towering trees. Striped by long, thin shadows, I felt like a bird in a cage. I looked back at Tamara. The shadow of a plane flickered over her.

The terrain was rugged. Hour after hour, day after day, we plowed through desolate woods, picked our way along rocky gorges, scaled steep, craggy slopes. Our bodies grew increasingly stiff and weary; our feet were blistered and bleeding from stumbling through briars and over sharp stones in our worn-out, ratty shoes. As we traveled, we searched for something—anything—to eat, now and then finding wild blackberries, dandelion roots, and mushrooms in the undergrowth. We slept under the boughs of fir trees, under jutting rocks, in rocky cul-de-sacs—once in a small cave.

The hunger, cold, and exhaustion—because of them, our minds began to wander. Sometimes Tamara and I had to hold hands just to make sure we didn't separate. Sometimes I saw things, and heard things: "Just come home alive, boy." That is what my grandpa had said to me at the station in Nuremberg when I'd left for the front. In my mind, I could see his face, and those of all my family.

In a valley we came upon the site of a small, long-forgotten battle, one that probably had taken place many months before. There had been, it seemed, no survivors—no one to bury the dead. Here and there, amidst the rocks and trees, lay skulls and whole soldiers of bone in ragged uniforms. Animals and insects had feasted on them; the weather had faded and rotted the uniforms white, indistinguishable. Broken and rusted weapons were scattered about, none of which were usable. In the moldering backpack of one of the skeletons, we found matches and tins of food. Bullets had pierced two containing what appeared to have once been plums; the contents were rotten. One tin was untouched. And upon opening it we found spiced ham. I immediately cut it in half, and we ate—gobbled it. I burped and immediately excused myself. "You have such fine manners—especially under the circumstances!" She laughed, then her eyes traveled the field of skeletons.

The boots of the dead were a little better than our own footwear. We threw away our worthless shoes and put on the best of the boots, stuffing them with rags to ease the pain in our feet and, because they were too large, to make them fit a little better.

I picked up the skull. "Thank you for the boots, friend. *Mein Freund!* Or are you Russian, *Karoshi druk?*"

Tamara, eyes sunken, laughed giddily.

I patted the uniformed skeleton on the back. "Thank you, Ivan! Or is it Heinrik?" I looked at his boots on my feet. "Good *German* boots, I see, Heinrik! Jackboots— hobnailed! The finest boots in the world!"

"I think we're going to end up as just two more piles of bones in this forest," said Tamara that night as we huddled by a small fire. She coughed raggedly.

It was with quiet surprise the next morning that we emerged from the trees to see rolling fields and farm- houses stretching far into the distance. One moment we were in one world; then, without warning, only half- believing it, we were in another. It seemed like a fantasy.

Near the tree line was a white, tidy farmhouse and a huge barn. A white fence surrounded a large pasture where cows and horses grazed.

A rising sun bathed the fields and farms in pinks and yellows.

A fantasy world—that is what it was. A pretty picture in my mind. Not until my hand pounded on a door did I hear and feel the reality.

The door opened a crack.

"Yes, what do you want?" demanded a middle-aged man in German, standing in the doorway, peering out at us. Behind him, a tall teenage girl looked at us over his shoulder.

"We've come a long way," I replied in German. "We are hurt, ill, and very hungry. We need help."

The man looked at us suspiciously. Our clothes were in tatters, blood had soaked through from our many cuts and scratches, and our hair was greasy and matted with dirt. I had a scraggly beard, and my throat was so dry and my lips so chapped it was difficult to speak.

"You are Russian," he said. "You wear Soviet army tunics!"

"Wir sind Deutsch." I told him that we were German, and tried to explain how we had come to be wearing Russian military shirts.

"I don't know who you are," he huffed. "Go away!"

The door slammed in our faces.

Behind the walls, the man and the girl began to argue. The girl wanted to help; the man, who seemed to be her father, wanted no part of us. "Either the boy's a deserter, or the two of them are Jews—who escaped from one of the camps. They can only bring trouble!"

Tamara and I were headed away when suddenly we heard a side door open. The girl rushed over and shoved an apple and half a loaf of bread in our hands.

"Thank you," Tamara said feebly.

"Where are we? What country?" I asked.

"Czechoslovakia, near Nachod," she said, and hurried back inside.

Eating the bread, we continued across a field, stumbling wearily over fresh-plowed earth. Not far from the first farm, we found a barn. No one seemed to be around. We made our way in, then up a ladder, and climbed far back into a cozy loft. Covering ourselves with hay, we fell into a deep sleep. When we awoke, it was to the sound of men's voices below. It was dark; faint light from a lantern moved along gray wooden walls. Terrified of being discovered, we scarcely breathed, let alone moved. Finally, the men left. When we were sure they were gone, we stole away into the night.

This became a pattern for us. We traveled at night, avoiding roads. From fields and gardens we took onions, strawberries, and potatoes. During the day we slept in barns, patches of woods, and haystacks—and once in a shed made of woven sunflower stalks. In the shed we found an old coat hanging from a nail and a heavy work-shirt covered with black grease stains: the coat went to Tamara, and I took the shirt. Not only did they provide warmth, but buttoned up tightly they also concealed our Soviet tunics. From our experience at the first farmhouse, it seemed clear that it was better to look like civilian refugees—which, in reality, we were—rather than in any way connected with the military, either German or Russian.

Tamara's cough all but went away for a time. Then it returned with renewed fury. Her head was hot to the touch, and her face was alternately flushed or ghostly pale. With each passing hour she grew sicker, weaker. I knew I had to do something. But what?

"I'm going to find a doctor for you." I told Tamara this as we hobbled along together one moonlit night across open ground.

"I'll be all right," she insisted, her words punctuated with coughs and her voice so faint and raspy I could scarcely hear her.

I did not press her on the matter. But my mind was made up. I could not let Tamara die. Despite the risk, we would enter the first village or town we came to and try to get her medical attention.

Later that night we saw a large convoy of military ve-hicles. Backlit by moonlight were troop carriers, trucks pulling light artillery pieces, and tanks. I guessed that they were Russian, which I would later learn to be wrong. They were German.

None of it seemed real. Suddenly I felt dizzy and unwell, and sat down—almost fell down. We crawled into a thicket; and watching the convoy, we fell asleep. I do not remember waking up. My next recollection is that it was daytime, and we were plodding along a dirt road. Everything seemed very dreamlike. My mind drifted. Space and time became disordered. I remember noticing a huge oak tree perhaps a hundred meters ahead. Suddenly the tree was not there. Turning around, I saw the tree some thirty meters behind us. I tried to force myself to concentrate, and thought I was succeeding. I wasn't. We kept passing things I had not noticed were ahead. An overturned tractor laying beside the road, a cow drinking from a trough, a girl on crutches—all of these things, and more, took me by surprise. A very old, bent-over man shuffled by and said good morning in German. I greeted him in kind. A horse-drawn cart with a peasant woman at the reins approached us. Ahead I could see the outskirts of a large town, and asked her the name of the place. She seemed frightened of me, and whipping her horse into a trot, hurried off as fast as she could go.

"Something's wrong with my head," I remember telling Tamara.

She muttered something, but I didn't understand her. And then she laughed and broke into a fit of coughing.

I was wondering what she was laughing about when I realized we were on a steep cobblestone roadway. Below was a large town. And nearby, up the road, was a very large, impressive-looking house surrounded by a high stonewall. Tamara and I sat down on a curbing. How long we sat there, I don't know. But I began to feel better and my mind seemed to clear.

"What do we do now, X?" Tamara asked.

"We'll go into town." I got to my feet.

Tamara looked up at me but continued just to sit there.

Puttering up the roadway came a strange-looking car. The thing was small, humpbacked in shape, the body domed in corrugated metal. At the wheel was a heavyset old woman. She brought the odd vehicle to a stop in front of a wrought-iron gate in the wall surrounding the house. She glanced my way.

"Could you please open the gate for me?" she asked in German, then repeated herself in a language I didn't know.

"Yes, ma'am," I answered, and then with considerable difficulty managed to open the twin halves of the heavy gate.

Tamara got to her feet. She was bone-thin, pale, and wheezing.

"You're ill," said the woman in her sort of lilting German.

Tamara, not understanding, looked to me.

I leaned forward, down to the open window. "Please help us," I said. "We are so tired and hungry and we can't think straight anymore."

"Who are you?"

"We are from a medical unit," I answered. "I don't know where any of the others are. I think most of them are dead."

Little blue eyes in a big pink face looked us over. Gears shifted raggedly. "Well, we can't have you dead, too!" she said. "Come, come. Get in the car."

We got in. The funny-looking car growled up the steep driveway, navigated a sharp turn, and then pulled to a stop in a pretty courtyard in front of a large, pinkish-looking stuccoed house.

Sanctuary

Elena Novak was the heavyset old lady's name. Her hair was dyed jet black; her small blue eyes, which seemed lost in her large, fleshy face, were intelligent and perceptive.

The town we were in, Klatovy, Czechoslovakia, she told us, had long been in German hands. Her son Gunter had been the mayor. When the Germans had taken over Klatovy in 1939, Gunter had tried to please everybody. He had tried to keep the townspeople happy. At the same time, he had to do the Germans' bidding and enforce their policies. A portion of all crops and factory products had to go to the German war effort; citizens had to provide free labor when asked to do so; open their homes as garrisons for German troops, and do so "in a friendly manner and with generous spirit."

There had been no serious problems . . . at first. But then Gunter, as mayor, had been ordered to identify all the Jewish residents of the town. The reason, according to a

German colonel: "We are trying to put a stop to the anti-Semitic conduct of some of our troops." At first, not knowing why the Nazis really wanted the information, he had complied. Shortly, on the orders of the Nazi high command, troops began rounding up Jewish people, confiscating all their possessions and then taking them away by train in cattle cars. News had trickled back about concentration camps and death camps. Gunter, sick with guilt over what he had inadvertently done, refused to continue helping the Nazis. For defying them, he was shot.

Mrs. Novak had once been a wealthy woman. But the Nazis had destroyed her life. After killing her son, they had taken most of her money and possessions, leaving her with only her strange little car and large house, which had been used as headquarters for officers. In fact, they had been there until only two days before we had arrived, when word had come down that the Russians were preparing an offensive to drive the Germans out of Czechoslovakia. German troops from Klatovy and from all the nearby towns had been sent to counterattack. The last large force from Klatovy had left the night before, and it was these troops—this convoy of men and weapons—that Tamara and I had seen the previous night.

Despite what they had done to her, Elena Novak did not hate the Germans—or anybody. She hated only the war. "I refuse to believe that all Germans are like the ones who killed my Gunter. I am of German ancestry myself, and so was my former husband and my son." She shook her head. "So tell me, how can I hate all Germans—when I am one myself?"

Mrs. Novak told us these things piecemeal and over a period of several days. Before learning her name or anything about her, I told her how ill Tamara was and how badly she needed a doctor.

"Elena will take care of everything!" she sang out in a confident, happy tone of voice as she headed off through a wood-paneled foyer toward a stairway. "But first we must get you cleaned up," she warbled. "Follow me upstairs, dears." I liked and trusted Elena right from the start, and so did Tamara. As we followed the seemingly irrepressibly happy old lady up the stairs, I smiled vacantly, feeling as though I had wandered into a strange, magical sanctuary.

In those days a bathroom was exactly that: a room to take a bath in, nothing else. Tamara went in first. I sat down on a little chair outside, waiting for her. I must have dozed off or drifted off into another world—because the next thing I remember I was in the bathroom, alone and taking off my filthy clothes.

The bath was so wonderful I almost drowned. Sitting in the warm, soapy water, I dozed off again—and woke up sputtering and gasping: I had fallen sound asleep and my head had slipped underwater.

A fluffy, baby-blue towel and fancy silk pajamas had been left on a stool for me. As I dried myself, I looked in a full-length mirror. An emaciated stranger looked back at me. I was extremely thin and covered with deep bruises and scratches, and my forehead, belly, and knee were scarred from wounds. My hair was long, and the stubble on my chin and cheeks had filled out and become a sparse, goatee-like beard. It was a face I had never seen before. Especially the eyes; they did not look like mine at all. They had a tiredly alert, hardened look, and seemed as though they belonged to someone much older. They were the eyes of a man, not a boy.

I put on the pajamas, and emerging from the bathroom, I looked through a half-open door into a bedroom. In the bed, sound asleep on her back, lay a beautiful young woman—Tamara—her long, dark hair framing her ivory face.

Footsteps clomped up the stairs.

"This was Gunter's room," said Mrs. Novak as she guided me across the hallway into a bedroom as large as our entire apartment back in Vilsburg.

I sat down on the edge of an enormous, canopied bed. As though I were a child, Mrs. Novak held a cup of warmed juice for me. She began feeding me pieces of buttered toast cut into little slivers. I felt silly. I wanted to protest and to tell her I could feed myself, but I didn't have the energy.

"You're handsome!" said Mrs. Novak happily. "As handsome as my Gunter—almost!"

"Thank you."

"You get some rest now."

"Tamara is very ill, Mrs. Novak. And—"

"I have an old friend in town who is a doctor. I will send for him." She smiled, patted my arm, and bustled away. "You just leave everything to Elena!"

Drowsily wondering at my good fortune, wondering why Mrs. Novak was so happy and being so good to us, I crawled under satiny covers and all but passed out. Never in my life—before or since—have I had such a wonderful sleep. I felt as though I was adrift in space in some sort of deep, luxurious stupor, now and then rolling over in complete contentment.

I slept nearly two days straight. From time to time, food was brought to me. I nibbled at it, then plunged back into a state of blissful unconsciousness. I only roused myself when the doctor arrived—an old man with graying red hair and a huge, lumpy-looking nose. He had already taken care of Tamara, and had given her penicillin for her fever and cough. Her numerous cuts and abrasions were painted with antiseptics then bandaged, and I was given the same treatment.

I gradually emerged from my torpor, as did Tamara. A very large, old-fashioned wardrobe was opened up to me; Mrs. Novak gave me the pick of all her son's clothing—suits, shirts, slacks—all of which were too large and hung on me as though I were a scarecrow. As for Tamara, all that could be found was the uniform of a former maid. But it fit her perfectly, and she looked very cute in it.

In the days that followed, Mrs. Novak doted on us. We had, it seemed, filled an empty space in her life. She treated me as though I were the son she had lost and Tamara as the daughter she had never had. I told her everything about the two of us, including the battle at Tarnapol, about ending up in the schoolhouse-hospital in Alreni, and how Tamara and I had worked together. I told her about the fighting that had erupted in Alreni while we were trying to evacuate, and about our long trek through Russia, the Ukraine, and Czechoslovakia.

"You must be very careful," Mrs. Novak warned me. "You could be shot as a deserter or a spy, and probably would have been already if you had arrived in Klatovy a few days earlier, before the German troops abandoned the town and headed east to try to stop the Russians."

To say the least, it was difficult for Mrs. Novak and Tamara to talk to each other. Mrs. Novak knew only a little Russian, and Tamara knew only the smattering of German I had taught her. I found myself serving as a translator, usually a pretty inept one. In Czechoslovakia, three languages were spoken—Slovak, Czech, and German. And the German spoken by Czechoslovakians was different in many ways from what I was used to back home. Often, Mrs. Novak and I ended up laughing as we struggled to communicate, and Tamara would join in, hardly understanding what it was we found so amusing, which made the whole situation even funnier.

In every way, those were happy times, great times—

some of the best of my life. It was as though all of us were in a private cocoon. For us, the war did not exist. Nothing existed outside the walls of that house. There was no one to bother us. No one to give us orders. There was no ugliness—or pain, or fear, or death.

Tamara steadily improved. Only a trace of her cough remained. My own strength returned. My knee bothered me, but other than that I felt fine. Food was in short supply, but there was enough to get by.

We knew, of course, that we could not stay in this cocoon from the world—in Elena Novak's house—forever. But after all we had been through, it was so tempting to make no move, and just stay there, letting the days slip pleasantly by. August faded, changed imperceptibly to September.

The house had been damaged by the troops and officers previously garrisoned there. Much of the furniture was stained and broken; carpeting was soiled; plaster walls were chipped and cracked where maps had been nailed. The gas, electricity, and phone no longer worked. Still, it was easy to see that it once had been a very beautiful home.

Tamara and I explored the place. It was so large and so different from the homes we had grown up in. One room became our favorite. At the end of a long, tiled corridor, it had been built in a grand manner, high-ceilinged and airy with a massive fireplace and French windows opening onto a large, unkempt garden. Mostly we stayed inside, content to sit on a sofa in that warm, sunlit room and gaze out at the garden and at the town of Klatovy in the valley below. At the base of a sweep of low foothills, dominated by a tall church, the town was beautiful; it looked like a picture postcard.

I will never forget that room. In there, Tamara and I, using one of the maps the Germans had left behind, plotted the course we would someday take to Switzerland, and eventually by ship to America. In there, we wrote letters to family and friends, not knowing when—or *if*—we would ever be able to send them, or even if those to whom we were writing were still alive. In there, we talked hour after hour, about anything and everything. About each other. And about the war, once having sort of a contest to see who could remember the most clichés—the largest number of tired aphorisms about the stupidity of war: "War is hell"; "There is never a good war"; "War is murder, with the blessings of the government."

I felt the last of these most strongly. "In peacetime, for killing someone, we're hung," I told Tamara. "But for killing during wartime, at the bidding of the same stupid government, they hang medals on us. It makes a great deal of sense!" I said sarcastically.

I went to a window, gazing at the world beyond the glass but not really seeing it. From behind, Tamara put her hands on my shoulders, then she rested her head against my back.

I turned. I ran a hand through her long, soft hair. Her

arms went around my neck. And as I pulled her closer, our mouths met. We kissed, softly at first, tenderly. For a moment, we stopped. I held her beautiful face with my hands, looking into her eyes, not sure I even believed what was happening.

Overrun

There is something dark and tangled in all of us—in all our souls; certainly, this is true of me. I understand it, but still I am ashamed of it. When Hals had died at Tarnapol, I had cried—but not just for him. I cried for myself, for my loss, and because I was ashamed: Deep down, I was glad it was he who had died and not I.

First in German, then in Russian, I confessed this late one evening, sitting in the parlor with Tamara and Elena.

"I feel so guilty," I said.

"You are not the first to do so," said Elena. She began talking about her son Gunter. He had been so plagued with guilt that, upon learning he was to be shot, he had not only accepted it with equanimity, but had expressed the feeling that he deserved to die. Elena continued on about the subject, about guilt, but was stopped midsentence. From far off came faint explosions. They continued for some time, then ceased.

"It's coming," said Elena. She turned to me. "I think the war has followed you."

———

We went to bed worried that night. The Germans had probably come face-to-face with the Russians and were now trying to stop their westward drive. The fighting sounded far off, but it was hard to tell exactly where it might be.

Little did we know that it was right around the corner—and would reach us before the night was through.

"Where are my hands?"

I never saw the German soldier who cried these words. But to this day I can still hear his voice. I can still hear the sound of trucks and other vehicles.

"Where are my hands?"

My eyes flipped open. It was near morning, but still pitch-black out. I was in Gunter's canopied bed. For a moment I lay there, staring groggily—and thinking of Willi, who had lost a hand at Tarnapol.

"Somebody shut him up!" yelled another voice in German.

I hurried to French doors opening onto a small balcony. Shivering in the dark chill before dawn, I stood in my bare feet on the cold tile of the balcony, watching a grotesque parade of German trucks and other vehicles. They were crowded with wounded soldiers, many crying in pain. I backed away, closing the doors on the sound.

"The Germans have been overrun by the Russians. They're retreating—in this direction! We must leave immediately!" Elena, Tamara on her heels, had burst into the room, a kerosene lamp in her hands lighting her face eerily. "Gather up what you can," she ordered. "Just the necessities, just what can fit in my car. Hurry!"

By the time we had dressed and were loading Elena's odd little car, Klatovy was coming under a barrage of Russian rocket and artillery fire. At first came long-range Soviet Seventeen-Twos; then "Stalin's Organs," multiple rocket-launchers, joined the bombardment. No shells or rockets were landing in our immediate vicinity, near Mrs. Novak's house on the hill overlooking the town. But we were trapped between the Russian rocket and artillery emplacements, somewhere to the rear, and the town, on which the shells and rockets were raining.

"Why are they doing this?" Elena cried.

The three of us could only stand and watch as the picturesque town was torn apart. The church steeple crumbled, its bell clanging dully as the sky popped open with blossoms of color and flying debris. Telegraph poles did splintering cartwheels and came crashing down in sparkling tangles of their own wires. Buildings ruptured from within, spewing bricks and shattered window glass into the street.

"Stop it!"

Over the terrible din, Elena shouted the same words over and over, her pudgy hands covering her ears, tears of rage and disbelief coursing down her pink-powdered cheeks.

To this day, I wonder what the Russians thought they were accomplishing by shelling Klatovy. The Germans were not firing back. In fact, there were no German troops there, at least none that I could see. The trucks carrying German wounded had already passed through. The only people in the town were civilians.

The bombardment tapered off, then ended. From below came the sounds of weakened walls collapsing, debris settling, and the hiss and crackle of countless fires.

"We have to go! Now is the time to go!" I told Tamara and Elena. "After the artillery comes the infantry," I said, parroting the words of Dobelmann. "They'll be coming— the Russians will. We have to get going—now!"

Elena just looked at me.

"Believe me, I know what I'm talking about!"

"I am not going," Elena said flatly.

In a desperate staccato of words, I told Tamara in Russian what Elena had said, and begged her to help convince her to change her mind.

By gesture, then by taking Elena by the arm and pulling, Tamara conveyed her feelings.

Elena kissed Tamara, then ruefully smiled at me. "I was born here," she said in German. "My life was here, and still is. I am an old woman." She turned and gazed briefly at the burning, battered town, then looked back at her house. "My home, by the grace of God, is still standing." She shrugged, a half-smile on her face. "The Russians will come and probably use my house and slop it all up. But the Russians can't be any worse than the Germans!"

"But anything could happen, Mrs. Novak," I exclaimed. "Please, you've got to come."

"Pazhalusta!" Tamara pleaded in Russian.

Elena shook her head, then removed a suitcase filled with her belongings from the car. "Now, you children go," she said. "Take the car."

"I can't drive," I told her.

"Shto?" Tamara asked what was happening and being said.

I explained about Elena's offer.

"I can drive," said Tamara. "My father used to let me drive a tractor."

I translated for Elena. Her big, loving arms went around us both. "You two, go. Quickly, now!"

We thanked her and kissed her good-bye.

"Hurry!" She waved us away.

After stalling out several times, Tamara finally got the car going. We all but did a free fall down the long, steep road leading to Klatovy, with Tamara riding squealing brakes the whole way. Reaching the bottom of the hill, we began weaving our way through the ravaged town, the streets an obstacle course of debris and craters. A riderless horse galloped on ahead, having an easier time of it than us. I saw several dead lying in the rubble, but miraculously, scores of people were emerging everywhere from cellars and the battered remains of buildings. A hand reached out toward the car. Tamara brought it to a lurching stop as a woman pulled the door open, then climbed into the back seat amidst food, clothing, and other items packed in there.

"Wait for my husband!"

As we started moving, a man crawled in through a window.

"Danke!" he muttered.

We left the town behind and were gaining speed on the open road. We began to pass small clusters of refugees. Most were on foot, some pushing baby buggies or pulling wagons piled with belongings. Angry, envious glances were cast our way, and we felt guilty: They were walking as we drove in relative luxury. "Rich scum!" I remember one man yelling at us.

Now and then we heard occasional rifle fire coming from a wooded area to our left.

We began passing horse-drawn carts filled with refugees and their belongings, and there was a solitary tractor. A bald man was sitting high in the driver's seat and a woman and child were clinging to the sides as it lumbered along.

The woman in the backseat began jabbering in German. "The next town is Grdnov. The railway runs through it. And we should be safe," she said, her tone upbeat. An instant later her mood darkened. "I don't think we have enough gasoline to make it that far," she said, looking over the seat at the instrument panel.

"No, we'll be fine, dear," said her husband, twisted up like a pretzel in the overfilled backseat.

Ahead, intersecting with the road we were on, was another road, this one clogged with people on foot and in vehicles of every sort, both military and civilian. We had almost reached the other road, and Tamara was slowing the car, when two men suddenly stumbled out from the woods. One, wearing a torn suit, was limping badly, using a rifle for support and dragging his bloody foot. The other, much younger, had a pistol.

"Halt!" he yelled in high-pitched German, the pistol aimed at the windshield.

The car crackled to a stop.

"Get out! All of you! Now!"

All of us scrambled out. A moment later the car was puttering away, the leg of the injured man sticking out a window.

Soon we had joined the other refugees headed toward Grdnov. We passed by a burning farmhouse, and in the distance, fields of rye and wheat crawled with flames. Behind a screen of smoke, the sun blazed, turning all the world a shadowy but oddly brilliant shade of blue. Blue hills. Blue trees. Even our arms and faces—and those of the other refugees—were blue.

As we plodded along, it quickly became apparent that, for the Germans, there had been disaster. Everywhere, they were in retreat. Trucks and armored vehicles began passing us. Bruised and bloodied soldiers rode, sitting desolately, their eyes remote, vacant. Other soldiers walked, singly and in groups—defeated and silent, nursing wounds, paying little or no attention to the civilians.

Now and then there were bodies beside the road, and abandoned vehicles. One was all too familiar: Elena's strange little car.

"It probably ran out of gas," I said.

Tamara nodded without looking at me. We continued walking.

Grdnov

A pall of dust hung over Grdnov. The town was choked with traffic of every sort. The depot, a large, dome-shaped structure, was in chaos. Soldiers and civilians were mixed together, cursing and yelling in anger, some weeping bitterly. A train was pulling out, with soldiers crowding every car, every compartment, and clinging to the sides like leeches.

"When is the next train?"

The question was being asked by countless voices in several languages, over and over—so many times it began to sound like a chant.

We would not wait for a train, Tamara and I decided. As did many others, we continued on through town, through streets teeming with people and vehicles, all moving in the same direction. Over the shuffle of feet and other noises came the rumble of a battle being fought somewhere to the north.

"Get out of the way or I'll shoot every one of you!"

People stood back as a German officer yelled and bullied his way through the crowd, waving a machine pistol. In his wake, from a heavy cart, came stretcher bearers with wounded soldiers. They made their way through the main door of what appeared to be a government building. From within came the cries of men in pain.

"We need doctors!" shouted the officer. He had entered the building only to reappear momentarily. He again waved his machine pistol and shouted to the crowd. "We need help, please. *Können Sie uns bitte helfen?*"

A few people glanced his way, then hurried on.

"Any kind of help! My men are dying!"

Tamara and I exchanged glances. She did not understand the officer's words, but it was obvious what he was asking. She grimaced as a horribly burned young soldier was trundled inside, then looked at me and nodded.

I touched the officer's sleeve. "We can help," I told him. "We were with a medical unit. We are not doctors, but we can be of use."

For a moment the officer seemed confused, as though he had not understood what I had said. Then his hard features softened. "Thank you!" Startling me, he put an arm around my shoulders. "And you tell them that Captain Gebhardt said you are to be fed!"

"Thank you, sir," I said, and then Tamara and I made our way inside.

We were in a triage area, where doctors were sorting out the wounded, deciding who could be saved and who could not, and who should be treated first. Much of the large room was filled with men on stretchers. Other wounded sat on the floor, mostly along the walls and aisles. Small, naked light bulbs hung from the ceiling over tables where doctors were operating.

"Why are you two just standing there? Get to work!"

A medic wearing rubber gloves, boots, and a blood-smeared rubber apron was glowering at us. Furious, he stormed off, then returned and shoved gloves and smocks into our hands. We put them on over our clothes; then we plunged into the work, washing and bandaging wounds, applying pressure bandages and tourniquets, splinting broken arms and legs.

We worked nonstop until about four-thirty, when food was brought in for the medics and orderlies. We were wolfing down potato soup and bread when I noticed a familiar figure striding toward us—Captain Gebhardt.

"Ah, my two volunteers!" he exclaimed in German, standing over us where we sat on the floor with our soup and bread.

I found myself looking at his knee-length black boots, then up at him, in his soiled gray uniform and visored cap with its edelweiss insignia. My chest tightened with fear: In reality, I was a deserter; Tamara a Russian, the enemy. For these reasons, both of us could be taken out and shot.

But Gebhardt was smiling benevolently. "I thank you again for helping."

"We are glad to do it, sir."

"Is the food at least edible?" He was looking at Tamara, asking her the question in German.

She smiled at him, trying to conceal her lack of understanding.

"She speaks only Slovak," I blurted, hoping the lie sounded convincing. "Tamara was a Czech volunteer with our unit."

Gebhardt was not listening, or even looking at us. He was gazing around at the sea of wounded men and boys. A change had come over him; he seemed lost in thought, and had a strange look in his eyes.

"How did this happen?" There was anger and great sadness in his voice. "The finest army in the world—reduced to this! And we have lost the war! How could we have lost?"

"I do not know, Captain."

He slammed a fist into his hand. "How?" Fury in his eyes, shaking his head, he wandered off.

Gebhardt was half out of his mind, I decided. Just as Mr. Long-Underwear and the other German soldiers in the bunker so many months before had been. The war had driven them crazy with rage, bitterness, and confusion. The Germans—especially the veteran soldiers—had been certain they would conquer the world. They had been led to believe—as I had—that nothing else was possible. But then the impossible had happened: They were losing, being driven back on all fronts. The British and Americans were attacking them from the west; the Russians were coming at them from the east, slaughtering them and driving them back to Germany.

Across the way, Captain Gebhardt was going from one wounded soldier to the next, patting each on the back and otherwise offering up encouragement. Most of the soldiers were very young. Words spoken long ago came to mind: "All the men are dead. Now they are sending us boys."

In the west, an oversize orange sun was dying as two other boys and I began digging in a sandy lot behind the government building. We were on burial detail. The bodies were brought out in children's wagons. We quickly dug shallow graves in the soft, almost sandy, soil, and then filled them in, leaving mounds.

To the north and east of Grdnov, heavy fighting was going on.

Headed into battle, troops of young German soldiers tramped past across the lot where we were working. I suddenly found myself staring. One of the leaders had a face that had been rendered easily recognizable by disfigurement. Dobelmann. As he trudged past leading his troops, like a teacher leading his students, Dobelmann's eyes met mine.

I do not know if he recognized me or not. He seemed to. But he just kept going.

Suddenly I thought of a friend. "Jakob!" I yelled.

My yell caused several heads to turn my way, briefly. But then they looked forward and continued on. One face kept looking back over a shoulder at me. There seemed to be a strange, enigmatic smile on the ruined, twisted mouth.

A train would be arriving soon.

Word spread quickly through the makeshift hospital; almost immediately we began transporting the patients to the domed depot, which was about a hundred meters distant and on the same side of the street. Stretchers, wheelchairs, gurneys, and carts—we used whatever was on hand to get the wounded to the train station.

There we waited. Day turned to night. Civilians, mostly Czechs and Ukrainians, milled about on the platform outside the depot anxiously gazing down the tracks, hoping at any moment to see the train. The tracks remained empty. From the north came the throaty grumble of battle.

By midnight the train had still not arrived. A misty rain began to fall. A few grimy, sopping-wet German soldiers straggled into the depot, directly from the front lines, it seemed. Their bodies stank; they were hollow-eyed, ragged, and radiated blood and death—and defeat. They began arriving in ever-increasing numbers. The hammering of automatic weapons fire erupted somewhere near the outskirts of Grdnov, and there was the occasional boom of artillery being fired, from within the town toward the advancing enemy. Now and then, to the northeast, came popping noises followed by *wooshing* hisses as parachute flares rose diagonally into the sky, paused for a moment, then slowly fluttered earthward, swinging like pendulums, lighting up the darkness with rocking white light.

The din of battle grew closer. Over it came another sound—the mournful shriek of a whistle. The sound was unmistakable. A train came into view, backing into the terminal. Crewmen, hanging from steel ladders on the cars carried lanterns, which cast yellow shadows all around. On top of each car were German guards with automatic weapons. Built for transporting cattle and other livestock, the sides of most of the cars were of wooden slats set far apart; wind and rain could stream in. The trip west would be a cold one. We didn't care. All we wanted to do was to get out of there before the fighting engulfed the town.

The depot came alive with activity. All medical personnel, including Tamara and I, went to work getting the wounded aboard. To the horror of the mass of civilians, German soldiers began herding them back, away from the train.

"They are just going to leave us!" a gap-toothed peasant woman cried shrilly.

An angry murmuring erupted from the crowd, and the people began pressing forward against the soldiers.

A single gunshot was fired into the air, silencing the crowd. "There will be room for everyone," said a German lieutenant in a loud but calm voice, a Luger pistol in hand.

"Be calm. You will be boarding soon. But as I am sure you can understand, the wounded must go first."

The crowd on the depot platform relaxed. They had the reassurance they needed. From a few of them came words to the effect that they could see the logic and fairness of what the officer had told them: Surely, the wounded had to be taken care of first. Some sounded ashamed of themselves for having been so selfish and untrusting.

We put most of the wounded on straw mattresses in the cars. Some of the soldiers arriving from the front helped us with the patients; however, most just climbed into the cars and found a comfortable place for themselves. Many immediately fell asleep; the rest sat staring into space, motionless as statues. Among the latter was a boy whose left leg was badly cut, and who suddenly went into convulsions. Tamara and I crawled into the car to try to help the doctor there. The convulsions ceased; the boy lost consciousness. By fluttering light in the car, I sprinkled sulfa powder on the wound, then watched as Tamara and the doctor stitched up the boy's flayed leg. I heard a commotion outside, on the depot platform. More soldiers climbed into our car, and into cars all up and down the line; at the same time, I heard the chug of the locomotive. The train rocked forward.

"They *are* going to leave them," I muttered aloud.

From outside, a German soldier rolled the heavy door of our car closed with a bang.

Through the slatted sides of the car I could see the

civilians on the depot platform, and caught a glimpse of more soldiers scrambling into cars. Other soldiers, with fixed bayonets, were herding the civilians back, away from the train as they yelled and begged to be let on board.

"You can't do this!"

They began to press forward.

"You're leaving us to die, you lying pigs!"

Overhead, from the roofs of the train cars, there were bursts of automatic-weapons fire, over the civilians' heads. Depot windows shattered and dusty plumes of stucco popped from walls. In a panic, the crowd retreated into the terminal building. As they did, the remaining soldiers raced for the train and jumped aboard.

Slowly it gathered momentum, leaving the depot and the civilians behind. Tamara and I looked at each other. Both of us were sickened by what had just happened. But there was nothing we could say, nothing we could do.

"Give me a hand."

We picked our way through the car to where the doctor was kneeling over a soldier with a badly infected foot. Tamara held up a flickering kerosene lamp. I pulled the boot and sock off. The doctor went to work.

Berlin

The train crossed the border into Germany sometime during the night. By noon—September 23, 1944—we were entering Berlin. Some parts of the huge, sprawling city seemed untouched; others had been pulverized by aerial bombardment, leaving acres of broken rock and cement. Passing through these sections, the train slowed to a crawl; and once we had to stop as the rails were cleared of debris and repaired. I gazed out the window.

A convoy of trucks passed by. Aboard them I saw what at first I took to be midget soldiers, but which I soon realized were children, boys with smooth, determined faces—being sent off to fight for what remained of Berlin. They looked to be only nine or ten years old. I was sixteen, an old man by comparison.

A woman hurried toward the train, a little girl wearing a green ballet costume in her arms. The child appeared to be dead.

———

We reached the Berlin depot untouched.

There, instead of unloading the wounded, we took on yet more patients, mostly German civilians. They took the places of soldiers still able to fight. These men, including the guards from the roof of the train, were formed into ranks. An officer informed them that they would be sent to strategic points in and around Berlin, such as supply dumps, bridges, and airports. At these places, they would join the *Volkstrum*—the civilian militia, which consisted of women, children as young as seven, and elderly men—to make a last stand against the encroaching Russians, British, and Americans. With blank expressions, they shuffled off like men condemned to death—which, in reality, was the case for most.

The train lurched. Tamara and the doctor and I began tending to the patients, especially the new arrivals. Our train was shunted to another line; and we were underway again, now headed south and out of the city. Soon we were clacking smoothly along through open countryside. From the open door of the car we saw farms, harvested fields, and country roads down which a few refugees were walking.

Our destination turned out to be a small village, a neat little hamlet tucked away in a wooded area. There, an aid station and a curious sort of hospital had been set up. Civilians and others helped us unload the wounded and get them situated—in houses. Every house in the hamlet, it appeared, had been turned into either a ward or operating room.

As we worked, whenever we had a chance, Tamara and I discussed what our next move should be. We'd leave the place; we'd escape it and head west, we decided. And doing so looked easy. There were no guards. There was only one officer, who was directing the operation, and a few wounded soldiers, earlier arrivals now recuperating in the place.

We waited until most of the wounded from the train had been unloaded; then, between us, Tamara and I lifted a young woman onto a stretcher. Her face and head wrapped in bloody bandaging, the woman kept begging us to tell her what had happened to her children. After laying her down on a sofa, Tamara patted the woman's hand. I told her that we would go and try to find out about her children.

"Thank you," she mumbled through her bandaging.

A nurse gave her a shot, and she was soon asleep. The two of us took the stretcher from the house. We leaned the thing against a wall, walked casually into the woods, then ran.

Dead

We slept that night in a woodcutter's shed. In the morning we talked over our plans. We would continue heading southwest. Vilsburg, my hometown, was in that general direction; so too was Switzerland, as well as the advancing troops of the Americans.

"We'll make it," I told Tamara.

"Of course we will, X."

It was early autumn, in the waning days of October; the elm, beech, and oak trees had already begun to drop their leaves, which crunched softly underfoot as we hurried along. The woods provided a degree of concealment, and safety. We kept to them as long as possible. But the trees thinned; then they were behind us, and we found ourselves on open road winding through farm country. There were other refugees, but only a few. Most were grim-faced and silent. A boy passed us on a bicycle, the tires of which were stuffed with grass. For a time we walked amidst a curious threesome. A humpbacked old man was pushing a baby carriage; in it, blue-veined legs hanging over the sides, was an old woman, probably his wife.

"I have rheumatism," the elderly lady told us. "I can't walk."

Alongside them, hands stuffed in his pockets, shuffled a teenage boy. "Why don't you leave us alone?" he snapped. "Get away from us!"

Perhaps an hour later we became aware of the delicious aroma of cooking meat. Our noses, and the babble of voices, quickly led us to the source. Around a bend in the road was a horse-drawn wagon. But the harness lay empty on the ground. The horse had been killed and cut up into steaks, now cooking on open fires around each of which several people had gathered.

"There's more than enough for everyone," said a tall man. "Take what you want. Otherwise it will just go bad."

Tamara and I ate ravenously. It had been days since we had eaten our fill, and neither of us could remember the last time we had had meat, except a little fish or pork in a thin soup.

After thanking the man, feeling stuffed, we continued on our way.

We passed the bombed remains of what had once been a large military training camp. About all that remained intact were wire fencing and a sign over a large gateway that, in German, read "Victory Forever!" Nearby was a fresh graveyard. I translated the sign for Tamara.

"If victory is death," I added, "then we have won."

We hurried off. About a half hour later, a misty rain began to fall. At first we ignored it, but soon we were getting soaked. We looked around for cover. There was none. Finally we saw a village looming ahead—and were sure it was our salvation. But as we approached the place we heard gunfire and then the *kruumf* of explosions.

Wanting no part of the bloodletting going on there, we headed across an open field. Scattered across it was the wreckage of an American bomber. Only the tail section was still in one piece. Tamara and I crawled in, and sat there, waiting for the rain to stop. It didn't. Instead it only came down harder, pinging overhead on the tinny metal and blowing into our faces through the jagged opening. It began to grow dark. Our cold, damp clothes glued to our bodies, shivering, hugging one another for warmth, we spent a miserable night.

The morning wasn't much better. It had stopped raining, but it was cold and dreary, and the field we were in had turned into a shallow, muddy lake. In water sometimes up to our knees, we slogged along for what seemed an eternity. Finally we reached higher ground. A feeble autumn sun came out; a cold breeze began to blow. Ahead, near the charred skeleton of a barn, we spotted an apple tree; hurrying to it, we found a single apple on a high branch.

As Tamara and I shared it, I remembered a freckle-faced boy, a friend, from what seemed a past life. Jakob. I could hear his voice: *"My father is an apple dealer. Our apples are shipped all over Germany!"*

"What are you thinking about?" asked Tamara.

I told her about Jakob, about the troop train, and about how his father was an apple dealer. "I don't know what happened to him, whether he lived or died," I said. "I hope he survived."

"So do I," said Tamara.

A thought turned my lips into a wry smile. "What," I asked facetiously, "a Russian caring about a German?"

"It just so happens that I am in love with a German!" she replied with mock adamance.

Tamara and I found a few overripe potatoes; we stuffed our pockets with them, and soon were on our way again. High overhead, endless clouds passed, looking like dirty rags being dragged across the sky. The sun went on and off, bathing us in sunlight one moment, in cold shadows the next. And then there was only shadow. Big, sloppy raindrops began to fall. I thought I heard artillery fire, but then realized it was the rumble of thunder; a spiderwork of electricity danced in the distance. Silver pins of electricity played across the underside of the cloud cover, then flickered out as the feeble pattering of rain rapidly gained momentum. Soon, we were being battered by another downpour, wind-driven rain flying almost horizontally into our backs, pushing us along. The road became a quagmire. Rain dancing on its hood, a black Mercedes passed us, its wheels looking like revolving balls of mud.

"Stop!" I yelled at the driver, who appeared to be the only occupant. "Give us a ride, please!"

The car kept going.

Ahead we spotted an umbrella. Red, fully open, and oversize, it was balanced in the branches of a tree beside the road. We hurried to it, momentarily under the impression that, by some peculiar stroke of luck, just the thing we needed had somehow been left for us. This silly notion was quickly dispelled. Crouching together under the umbrella was a young woman and a little boy. Though wrapped in a blanket, the two were shivering terribly— and looked even worse off than us. We gave them two potatoes. The little boy stared at his as though he had never seen one before. The woman smiled wanly. *"Danke schön,"* she said, then whispered something into her little boy's ear. He smiled brightly. *"Danke schön!"* he piped in a babyish voice, echoing his mother and obeying her whispered request to say thank you.

We saw no one else before reaching the town. The place took us by surprise; night had long since fallen, and most of the time we'd been walking with our heads down, as if in surrender to the rain. One moment we were tromping forlornly through muck, our feet heavy with mud; the next we were on a paved highway, the black-against-black skyline of a town looming ahead.

"Thank God!" Tamara, her wet hair plastered down against her head and face, squeezed my hand.

Gathering our energy, we quickened our pace. The leather sole of my left shoe started coming loose, and soon was flapping against the pavement.

The town was a strange-looking place, an odd mixture of modern and medieval buildings, ancient church spires mingling with factory chimneys, derricks, and billboards. All was quiet, and in the dark and rain, the place gave the impression of being deserted. As with other towns, some sections seemed relatively untouched while others had been shattered into slabs of broken concrete by bombing raids.

"Which way?" asked Tamara, her teeth chattering.

I shrugged wet shoulders, and then led the way, not having the slightest idea as to where I was going.

We made our way along cobblestone streets, the only sounds the wet crunch of our footsteps—and the flapping of my left sole. Through drifting curtains of fog and rain, we spotted a small hotel. From the outside it looked in good shape, but as we pushed our way inside we found that, beyond the front wall, hardly anything remained of the place. What had once been the lobby now consisted of busted chairs and other junk floating in a huge, water-filled crater. Above what was left of the registration desk hung a banister from which broken spindles dangled.

Out in the rain again, one street over, we came to a bleak row of storefronts, among them what was left of a barbershop. Entering the place, I almost jumped out of my skin. Coming toward me was a man. I stopped. He stopped, and I realized I was looking at my own dark reflection in a remnant of a wall mirror. I turned, and taking another step, stumbled over a body—that of a German officer lying facedown between two barber chairs.

"Dead," said Tamara, feeling for a pulse.

We took from the body only what we could use, items we desperately needed; still, I had the disturbing feeling I was robbing one of my fellow soldiers. I pulled off his heavy gray-green coat, then helped Tamara into it. The thing engulfed her. A pistol lay nearby; I wanted no part of it, but I took the dead man's boots and wool shirt. I began to worry. The officer, who had been killed by a wound to the side of the neck, was still relatively warm.

"By the looks of him he has hasn't been dead long," I told Tamara. "There's been fighting in this part of town, and not very long ago. We should get out of here."

She nodded.

I looked out into the street through a little waterfall pouring off a doorway awning. All was dark and still.

Bundling up as best we could, we picked our way along the cobblestone street through the sodden, dead-looking town.

A hand touched my shoulder. "Look," whispered Tamara.

In a nearby building a light glowed eerily in a window, then suddenly went off. Tamara turned to me, a questioning look in her eyes.

"Something's wrong," I said softly.

We backed away, then headed up a winding side

street—nervous, moving slowly and warily. At first I wasn't sure what I was hearing. I held up a hand. Tamara stopped. Over the gurgling of water flowing down a gutter came the sound of muted, small voices. A hiss for quiet. The voices abruptly stopped; in the same instant, I stared, paralyzed by fear. In the ruins of a storefront, I saw movement . . . and saw a helmeted form in silhouette behind the black, wet barrel of a machine gun.

"Ach! Nein!" I gasped.

All changed to slow motion. Tamara, a short distance ahead of me, was turning. I reached out my left hand for her, as the black of night was speared red with machine-gun fire. Tamara shrieked as she was knocked backward— and away from me. My arm and face exploded with pain. Screaming, blood spilling from my mouth, I stumbled forward a step, then fell.

"Cease fire!" someone yelled in English.

In agony, I struggled to my knees. The machine gun was silent. Dark forms were coming toward me. I felt a pair of hands search me for weapons as another hand came to rest on my shoulder.

"Hang in there, buddy," said someone in the tough, strangely accented English I had heard in American movies.

"They're just kids—civilians," said someone else. "Dammit!"

The barrel of a rifle pointed at me was lowered. A soldier, an American flag insignia on one shoulder, frowned grimly.

Dead

The left side of my face hurt horribly and I was having trouble seeing out of my left eye. I tried to reach up to touch the eye but found that for some reason I couldn't.

"Pull back," a soldier ordered, getting to his feet. "Get 'em outta the street."

A shock wave of horror hit me. I slowly turned. A short distance behind me lay a coat-covered bundle. Tamara.

"Dead," said someone.

I tried to cry out. It was impossible. My mouth was full of blood; I started to gag as I opened it.

"You heard the lieutenant," said a soldier, looking around apprehensively, rifle in hand. "Pull back. Now!"

A hulking helmeted silhouette went slowly past, a coat-bundled form in his arms.

I spat blood. My words were garbled, but I managed to say the only thing that mattered. "Tamara!" I shrieked.

Narcissus

I was dreaming I was hanging from something by my left arm. The arm felt as though it was being pulled out of its socket. It hurt horribly. People were asking me questions, but all I could remember is that I was supposed to say that I didn't remember. And this time it was true: I really didn't.

I blinked awake, lying propped up in hospital bed. The dream evaporated. With my right hand I touched a thick mask of white bandaging covering my head. Through eye slits I could see patients in white gowns, and white-sheeted beds and nurses in crisp, white uniforms. White. Everything was white in that hospital. I wondered how I had gotten there.

"He's coming around," said somebody in English.

I'd heard the same words—a similar statement—long ago. I tried to remember where.

My head hurt. My face hurt, and I could not see much out of my left eye. But mostly it was my left arm that hurt.

I tried to move, to sit up straight. Traction pulleys jangled. I screamed in pain.

An oversize face loomed close to mine. A nice face, that of a nurse with little glasses perched on her nose.

"Please, the pain!" I cried—in German . . . then English . . . then Russian, my voice sounding funny, garbled.

The nurse said something to me. She bustled about. I felt sheets pulled aside, and then the cooling sensation of alcohol on my shoulder, quickly followed by the sting of a needle.

"That should do the trick," the nurse said in American English.

Her footsteps tapped away. A doctor walked by. I followed him with my eyes, but the vision in my left eye was still blurry. I began to feel a little woozy, and much better—except I knew that something was terribly wrong, that something awful had happened, but I couldn't remember what. My face felt numb, the pounding in my head had stopped, but my left arm, though the pain had faded, continued to throb.

Unable to see much of anything out of my left eye, I turned my head to see out of my right. I looked at the traction wire hanging from an overhead bar, and at my left arm. Only there was no arm. From a few inches below the shoulder, it was gone.

———

The town of Lathenow, Germany—that is where it had happened, I learned later. A machine-gun blast had shattered my left arm; one bullet had entered my open mouth and exited my left cheek; the heavy-caliber bullets had also ricocheted and splintered, and fragments of stone and steel had hit me in the head and face, mostly on the left side. My left eye had been abraded. At the American Red Cross hospital in Stasfurt, Germany, where I had been taken, my left arm had been amputated, and more than a hundred stitches had been needed to close the wounds to my scalp, forehead, and left cheek.

When I first regained consciousness in the hospital, I only knew that I had been badly injured. Then came the horror of finding that my arm was gone. I had seen so many others with missing limbs, and I'd thought I'd understood what they had been feeling, what they had been going through. But I had understood nothing—not until it had happened to me.

The wounds to my face were serious, but they would heal, I was told, and the vision in my left eye would probably return to normal. But my arm—all I could think about was my arm—and the unimaginable, unacceptable reality that it was gone. In drugged sleep, I often dreamed that it was still there, always to awaken to the awful truth that it was not. I would turn away from it, from the stump, and look emptily through eye slits at the ward, thinking back.

More and more, I began remembering the incident. I remembered the machine gun firing, and right before that, hurrying up a cobblestone street, shiny with wetness. Strangely, my recollection was of being alone, of being by myself when the shooting started. It seems incredible to me now, but for days, as I lay there in the hospital, I did not remember Tamara being killed. I did not remember her at all. Not even her name.

Even when I was told that a girl had come to see me— even that did not stir the slightest recollection. But then I heard her voice. Through the eye slits I saw her, a bandage on her head, black, raccoon-like circles around her eyes. I gasped, and then began to cry. I remembered her. She was dead. Unbearable grief at losing her overwhelmed me. Incredibly, I was looking at her when the impact of her loss hit me for the first time.

"You're dead," I mumbled through the mouth slit in my bandages, even as I said it realizing that it wasn't true.

"X!" Tamara was holding me, sobbing.

My right arm went around her shoulders. What remained of my left arm was stopped by the traction wires. Restrained by them, the stump, seemingly with a mind of its own, rattled noisily as it too tried to reach for her.

Tamara came to see me every day. She told me that a bullet had grazed her head, knocking her cold. When she'd come out of it, with only a concussion and two black eyes, she had repeatedly asked after me. At first, no one had understood her. Two days had passed before a Russian-speaking nurse had found out that Tamara was only one floor up from me, in the women's ward.

She fussed over me. She took care of me. She chattered, her eyes averted from my stump of an arm. I didn't mention it, and perhaps for that reason, neither did she. I said little. And I began to get irritable, annoyed, angry. I didn't want to hear her voice. It grated on me. And I did not want her there. I didn't want her pity. I didn't want to see her—or, really, her to see me.

One afternoon she was helping feed me. A little broth dribbled from the opening around my mouth and into the gauze. Furious, I cursed, and with my right hand sent the tray of food flying.

"Clean it up!" I yelled. "Then get out!"

The next morning I told the nurses I did not want Tamara to be allowed to visit. Later I heard Tamara at the door to the ward, first arguing, then crying. I looked over at her as a nurse came to talk to me. Before she said a word, I asked her to tell Tamara that I was sorry for what I had done but that I needed to be alone.

The nurse headed away. I turned my head. I saw Tamara and two nurses talking. I looked away. When I looked back, she was gone. One of the nurses was frowning across the way at me.

———

November 1, 1944: An American soldier in the bed next to mine died that day. Envy—that's all I felt.

I began receiving notes from Tamara. Desolation, emptiness—that is what they caused me to feel. Once, I wept; I cried for all that was lost, and what might have been. A little stack of her notes began to grow on the table at my bedside. I couldn't throw them away—any more than I could bring myself to write back.

"You have a letter," said a nurse one morning.

"Just put it on the table," I said, thinking it was another note from Tamara.

"It came by military post; it's from your mother."

"My mo-mother?" I stammered, certain it was from Aleksandr's mother, and feeling as though I was reliving an ugly moment from the past. "But how would she know I'm here?"

"The girl contacted your family."

I looked at the postmark; the letter was from Vilsburg. "Please read it to me," I said.

"'My darling Erik,'" the nurse began. "'It was the most wonderful moment of my life when I learned that you are alive! I know that you have been badly hurt, but time heals all wounds, as they say. I would give anything to come see you, but travel is impossible right now, as I'm sure you understand.

"'Some bad news: I am sorry to tell you that your grandma has passed away. Fortunately, she died peacefully in her sleep, and for this I am thankful to God. I was afraid that losing her would kill Grandpa. He was so depressed, so lost. But the news that you are alive has restarted his life! He is filled with energy, and can't wait to see you! Love, Mother.'"

I was crying and smiling at the same time. The nurse put the letter on the table, then squeaked away on rubber-soled shoes.

Early one evening my arm was taken out of traction. Wires were slowly lowered. The stump of my left arm was cleaned and rebandaged. It hung useless at my side. I moved it, raised it, stared at the thing in disgust, and wondered what had been done with the amputated hand and arm. A vision passed through my mind, a remembered image: Seen through an oval-shaped window on the troop train, a young woman walked toward an incinerator, a human leg in her arms.

Two or three days later came a moment I was dreading. There were two nurses and an American doctor. I remember that the doctor had unusually small hands.

"Keep in mind," he said, "that the healing is not yet complete. The wounds to your face were severe, but in time . . ." He left the sentence unfinished; then, with his small hands, he began unwinding my head mask of gauze. There seemed to be miles of the stuff. He and the nurses began snipping and pulling the stitches—carefully and slowly, seeming to be taking forever to get all of them out.

"I'd like a mirror, please," I said when they had finished.

The doctor exchanged glances with the nurses, and then nodded. One of the nurses left; the mirror she returned with was a feminine one, of the kind a lady would have on her dressing table. It was heart-shaped and had a pink handle and frame, and a red backing. For a long while I stared at the plastic red back of the thing. Then I turned it over and saw my face. My left eye drooped beneath a deep scar that snaked across my forehead; my left cheek looked like someone had carved a hideous design in the flesh; and part of my jaw had a sunken look to it.

"It's not so bad," said one of the nurses. "Really."

I handed the mirror back to her, then asked the three of them to leave.

I continued to refuse to let Tamara in to see me. And then I wrote her a long letter in which I told her I wanted her to be happy and go on with her life without me. I wrote that I would always love her, always remember her, but too much had changed, and it was better that we go our own ways.

The next morning I awoke to find her standing at the foot of my bed.

"I love you," she said, and then walked out of the ward.

I wanted to call to her to come back. I didn't. Instead, numb inside, sick with grief and self-pity, I just lay there, staring at nothing.

That afternoon I was taken in a wheelchair out to a garden area to get some sun and air. Narcissus. I can still smell the aroma of narcissus, and of pine trees and fresh-mown grass. And there was a trellis-like fence on which a flowerless vine grew. I saw only nurses and other patients, at first. And then I saw Tamara, standing there quietly by the fence, wearing a blue dress, and with a white ribbon in her hair.

I turned my head, covering the left side of my face with my one hand. I wanted to scream. I wanted to run.

She sat down beside me. I felt the touch of her finger-tips on my right arm; and then she gently pulled my hand from my face. "I love you," she said. Her soft lips touched mine.

I tried not to, but I couldn't stop myself. I hung my head and cried—for myself, for everyone, and for all that had happened. Tamara's arm went around me, and then her head was on my shoulder.

Epilogue

On May 7, 1945, Germany surrendered. On March 21, 1946, my eighteenth birthday and two years after leaving for the front, Tamara and I were married—in a chapel in Vilsburg—the town itself having remained mostly untouched by the war. Only the congregation at my wedding had been touched: Among them were there were many widows and widowers, and many cripples—other men and women like me. Tamara wore a simple white dress, a bouquet of narcissus in her hands. My mother and grandfather were there. They beamed with great joy.

Three years later, Tamara and I arrived in America. From New York we moved to Fort Worth, Texas, and from there to Seattle, Washington. After just arriving in Seattle, we learned Mother had remarried, and Grandpa was living with them, and the three had refurbished and reopened the *Küche Apfelsine*. After less than three years, Tamara became a registered nurse at a Seattle hospital, then went on to run a free clinic. We have three grown children—Hals, Nikolai, and Katerina Elena. Katerina, who is as beautiful as her mother, is a doctor. Hals is a social worker. Nikolai is an artist, a sculptor.

For many years I taught history and languages. Now I am retired, as is Tamara, though we both sometimes volunteer our time at the clinic. Often, in the evenings, we take long walks together in the woods, usually along the shoreline of the lake near our home. It was during one of these walks that Tamara suggested I write this book.

At first I refused to even consider it, mostly, I think, because the memories are so painful. Little by little, she changed my mind. She convinced me to put into writing what happened. With patience, she explained to me the reasons why she believed it had to be done, and why this strange—and sometimes ugly—story had to be told.

Author's Note

This is a work of fiction based on the lives of two very remarkable people. Though names, dates, and places have been altered whenever necessary, the story is not only true, but also loosely parallels the experience of an estimated thirty thousand German soldiers during World War II on the Eastern Front. A great many were trapped behind Russian lines. Some of the wounded were given medical attention; others were literally thrown out of Russian hospitals and left to die. A great many—wounded or not—were executed; some were imprisoned and enslaved. A few were able to blend into Russian society or flee to neutral, friendly nations.